Shout the Call

Lucy Onions

Lucy lives in Walsall with her husband, daughter, one mad dog and a grumpy rabbit.

Also by Lucy Onions:

Good for Nothing

And if the Sun Comes Up

Copyright © Lucy Onions, 2015

The right of Lucy Onions to be identified as the author of this work has been asserted in accordance with the Copyright, Designs and Patents Act 1988.

All rights reserved. No part of this publication may be reproduced, stored in a retrieval system, or transmitted in any form or by any means, electronic, mechanical, photocopying, recording or otherwise, without the prior permission of the publishers.

ISBN-13: 978-1514771815

ISBN-10: 1514771810

For:

Simon, Molly, Mom, Dad, Ella, Paul and Max. I couldn't do any of this without you all.

Chapter 1

The bedside clock let out its shrill alarm, notifying me it was time to get my backside out of bed. It had been set for six thirty am, religiously, ever since I started my job at New Music; Non Stop as a feature writer, reviewer, interviewer and photographer (the latter being for my own business first and foremost and the magazine second).

Within eighteen months of working at the magazine, I'd covered some of my favourite bands; not bad at all when you consider I've never had any formal training or have any qualifications for it.

I got the job out of my "pure passion for music and how it makes me feel," according to our editor, Hanley James. Apparently, the music reporting industry need more like me.

I turned my laptop on, swiftly followed by my phone. Luckily, I've never been the kind of person who feels the need to leave my mobile on overnight; even that muted buzz of silent mode was enough to totally disturb a decent night's sleep. I entered my password when my laptop prompted and left it to load up; it was time for my morning shower.

After a brief yet refreshing wash and spruce up, I headed back to my bedroom and plonked myself down on my faux-antique chair in front of my faux-antique dressing table, dragging my index finger over the mouse pad. The laptop screen burst into life after lying in dormant standby. Another ritual; every Monday morning I check my inbox and it's always crammed full. I work ridiculous, unsociable hours, especially over the weekend and Monday is usually my one, easy day. I can't grumble though; who else can say they get paid for doing something they absolutely adore? I opened my email account to a barrage of junk mail; shockingly, there were only two from work.

FROM: hanjames@nmns.co.uk

TO: beaharvey@nmns.co.uk

SENT: Sunday, 10:27

SUBJECT: You're not going to believe this……..

Hey Bea

Sorry its short notice but you're going to be out of the office ALL of this week unless I tell you otherwise.

Let's just say, I've managed to bag AAA for one of your favourite bands ever but I'm not telling you who it is just yet as there are a few loose ends to tie up. Once everything's confirmed 100%, I'll mail you again. Man, if this comes off, it's going to be HUGE – for us and for you!

Catch ya later

Hanley xxx

Oh my God; it couldn't be, could it? I opened the second email almost immediately.

FROM: hanjames@nmns.co.uk

TO: beaharvey@nmns.co.uk

SENT: Sunday, 13:09

SUBJECT: You're not going to believe this…….

Hello again, my beautiful Bea

So, you want the good news or the even better news first? Nope, don't answer that. Here goes:

You know how I thought it'd be just one week out of the office for you? Well, it's just turned into six. You'll be the official tour photographer/reviewer/general 'jack-of-all-trades' for ……….. SHOUT THE CALL! Basically, you need to pack, like yesterday! Like I've already said, I really am sorry for the late notice on this but I wouldn't have given this gig to anyone else, Bea.

Can you call me as soon as you get this? You'll need a pen and paper or something to take down a few details. I won't email you with further info; you'll be asleep before you read to the end.

Speak soon

Hanley xx

I couldn't do anything but stare blankly at the screen. The minute I came to, I grabbed my phone, found Hanley's number and hit call.

"Hanley."

"Hey, Bea," Hanley replied, sounding excited, "so I can assume you got the emails?"

"Um, yeah and wow; Hanley - I don't know what to say."

"Look, you can thank me and all that when you get back. Have you packed yet?"

I immediately felt bad.

"Ah, sorry – no," I replied guiltily, "I only just picked up my mail. I haven't had chance to all weekend - it's been chaotic. I only had an hour or so to relax yesterday and I just slept."

"Okay, hon, doesn't matter," Hanley replied, sounding a little irritated but not angry. "Anyway, you can pack in a minute. Here's the deal: the band's management will meet you in The Britannia at Euston Station.

"They're only based in Camden so I've told them you'll give them a call when you get there. You'll be doing your very first interview with Shout the Call, there – in the pub.

"By all accounts and according to Jim Stanley, the manager, they enjoy a pint or ten. You'll then be heading back to their shared house in Camden and then tomorrow you'll be out on the road with them. All expenses covered, Bea. Apparently, the band's lead singer has asked for you specifically. He loves all of your work, honey. Well done!"

I was flabbergasted. Aaron Holmes, lead singer of Shout the Call, wanted me - albeit just on a professional basis. Any basis at all is good for me.

"Honestly, Hanley; I just don't know what to say!" I replied.

"Well, I'm guessing you'll have plenty to say later at

the interview." Hanley said, "I know you know a ton about the band already but I suggest you get your research up to date and your questions sorted on the train honey. You know the drill; keep it relevant, edgy and to the point. Make it yours. Now, any questions?"

"Nope" I replied honestly because I didn't, not even one. I still couldn't quite believe what I'd just heard and even with the scribbled notes I'd made on a page of my reporter's notebook, I couldn't get my head around it.

Chapter 2

It felt like I had packed the entire contents of my flat into my case as I lugged it off the escalator and spotted The Britannia. I wiped the sweat from my brow and the hair that had stuck itself to my clammy head. Thank God I was meeting the band in a pub; there was a pint of cider with my name on it and it seriously would not touch the sides.

I found a booth big enough to accommodate us all in a rather snug little alcove. I heaved my case under the table, pulled my phone from my back pocket and phoned the number Hanley had given me for Jim Stanley.

"Hi. Is this Mr Stanley?" I asked into the phone.

"Sure is," came the reply, "Is this Beatrice Harvey

from New Music; Non Stop?"

"It is indeed," I replied nervously. "Um, just to let you know that I'm at The Britannia now."

"Well, Beatrice," Jim replied, "thanks for phoning through oh, and by the way, please call me Jim. Let's start this shindig as we mean to go on."

"Oh, okay. Thanks, Jim," I said, immediately feeling at ease.

"We'll be with you in fifteen, maybe twenty minutes. See you in a bit."

******

The band's arrival couldn't come quick enough. I was almost salivating over that first, refreshing gulp of a pint but in the meantime, best to let Hanley know I was okay.

"***Hey, Hanley***," I began the text, "***I'm here. Spoke to Jim. They're on their way.***"

Hanley replied almost instantly.

"***Cool, Bea. Glad you got there OK. Now I know***

you're there to do a job but just try and enjoy yourself and go with the flow. They love a good time so take a leaf out of their booze soaked books. You haven't got to drive or anything, so it's all good!"

"*I know,*" I tapped back, "*Thanks again Hanley*"

I pushed my phone back in my pocket and spotted a face (and then the rest of his body) that I knew, without doubt, was Aaron Holmes, lead singer of Shout the Call. It was the face of the man I had pretty much obsessed over for as long as I could remember, and of course, was old enough to.

It's always amazed me how he never seems to look any older, and now, seeing him in the flesh, his blue/green eyes and nape-of-the-neck tousled curls - medium brown with hints of dirty blond, I almost failed to notice the rest of the band filing in behind and sitting down.

"Ah, finally we meet, young Beatrice," a man, who I assumed to be Jim Stanley due to our earlier telephone conversation, extended his hand. I immediately shook it.

"Cool name. I like it." Aaron piped in, uninvited.

"Um, thanks," I replied, hoping that the hue of crimson red flushing my cheeks wasn't as ridiculously apparent as it felt. "Actually, I'd feel more comfortable if you called me Bea. Beatrice sounds so 'old'."

"You do?" Aaron replied, "Well I think it's gorgeous and it really suits you. You ROCK your name!"

I was lost for words.

"You okay?" Aaron asked.

I hoped the shake of my head was just a figment of my imagination but it seemed it wasn't, as Aaron's laugh pointed out.

"Beatrice. Hello?"

"Oh, um, sorry," I replied quickly once I'd come round from my little daydream.

"You want a drink?" he asked, miming the act of drinking as if I didn't understand. *Finally*, I thought, *it's about bloody time.*

"I'll have a pint of cider, please," I answered as he got up and made his way to the bar. I snatched my gaze away from him in time for Jim to make the proper introductions.

"Guys, this is Beatrice Harvey, or Bea, as she prefers to be known. Aaron already knows of her. He was the one who actually pointed her sterling work out to me."

Aaron shot me a smirk. I gulped and wondered if it sounded as loud as it did in my head. Jim continued.

"Anyway, Bea works for New Music; Non Stop and I've been told she's a great all-rounder," Jim suddenly stopped, tutting as the band laughed like little school boys at their self made innuendo.

"Oh, behave yourselves," Jim went on, "Bea is a top photographer, reviewer and interviewer and according to her Boss, she's the best in the company. She's going to be joining us on the entire tour, which means she'll be on the tour bus for the duration, and any hotels we stay in here and there. Any questions?"

Alex Henry, Shout the Call's bassist, was first in line.

"Where's she going to sleep?"

"With me, I hope!" Aaron answered, walking back towards us with a round tray full of drinks.

"Now now," Jim said, stopping the conversation before it had chance to even begin, "come on lads, I wasn't born yesterday! Bea," Jim looked straight at me, directing his speech, "You'll have your own bunk but sadly you'll be sharing the space with this bunch of reprobates. If anything goes on that you're not happy with, anything at all, you just come to me, okay?"

I nodded, staring intently at Jim but at the same time, feeling Aaron's eyes boring into me.

"So, are we all clear?" asked Jim, directing the

"Yeah, we know that but you heard what Jim said; the action don't start until tomorrow night which gives us all plenty of time to nurse our bad heads, eat a load of shit and then get back on it again until we hit France."

"Yeah," Aaron agreed, "c'mon, honey; don't spoil it. Let's have fun. Let's get wasted!"

I should have been angry at being called "honey" by someone I barely knew but I wasn't. The hottest lead singer I had ever set my eyes on said it and it sounded so good. *What the hell*, I thought to myself, *go for it*. I had a feeling it was going to be a long night.

******

"I really, really need to go now," I addressed the band, totally aware of how slurred my speech sounded; "I've had way more than I should and I'm tired."

The band playfully mocked me, repeating my words in a whining manner.

"Look, I'm not a lightweight," I shot in defensively, "I'm just being sensible. I'll flag a cab down outside; I already have your address." I stood up unsteadily and tried desperately not to tumble over as I shuffled out of the booth. A quick look at the clock again told me it was seven thirty. We'd been drinking and chatting for the best part of six hours.

"Hey, Bea," Aaron said between hiccups, "I'll come with you. I'm done here too."

"No, it's okay, Aaron, really. You don't have to leave on my account. I'm a big girl. I can take care of myself."

"I don't doubt that but I've had more than enough too." Aaron replied.

"Okay, cool," I replied, "At least now I'll have some company in the taxi."

"Taxi; what taxi?" Aaron replied with a guffaw, "We're walking. It'll be a good way to get to know each other a bit."

I smiled awkwardly and felt blood rush to my cheeks again. He smiled back and we walked out of the pub.

******

We didn't speak for a few minutes or so. I could sense he was itching to break the ice but he couldn't quite crack the surface.

"So, I don't know whether you know this," I said, deciding to take the lead, "but Shout the Call are my favourite band ever!"

"Serious?" Aaron replied shyly.

"Totally," I answered with possibly more gusto than was really needed. "I've seen you live eleven times and I have all three albums; all your singles and your b-sides too. Oh, and you won't believe the amount of merch I have."

I realised quickly that I sounded more like a crazed fan-girl rather than a well-rounded, grown up but then, that's the story of my life; music will always be my passion. It's probably the only thing that excites me anymore. Aaron didn't need to know this though. I was here on business.

"Shit. Sorry, Aaron. You see; this is what drink does to me," I went on, feeling silly, "I can talk for England anyway; that's probably one of the reasons I got this job. Add alcohol to the equation and well, it's like I've had an intravenous caffeine injection."

"Hey," Aaron quickly replied, "keep your apologies. I've read a ton of your reviews and your interviews are perfect; just the right mix of formal and fun. There aren't many that do that, you know. I can't begin to tell you how many planks we've had sitting in front of us asking the same old, generic shit. It becomes a script in the end."

"It should never be like that!" I interjected.

"Exactly, Bea and that's why I sounded Jim out about you. When I read your work, your reviews especially, I can feel your excitement or, in some cases, boredom. You've never slated a band but you know when something needs work and, as I've already said, your interviews are just incredible. I love them. It's more like reading a chat between friends. Your passion for music comes across in everything you write. That's why I wanted you to cover this tour, Bea."

"Thank you, Aaron," I gushed, "that's such a lovely thing to say."

Aaron smiled awkwardly and looked down, shoving his hands in his pockets.

"It's actually not the only reason I want you on tour with us, Bea," he said, his voice dropping lower to almost a deep growl, "I've seen your personal Facebook and Tumblr pages; I'm seriously liking the photos. I've read your bio and your blogs. I like what I see. I like it a lot. Sorry, that sounds way too intense and weird, doesn't it?"

"Um, yes - I suppose it does, a little," I replied, "but then again, I've idolised Shout the Call for as long as I can remember and I may have just a very small crush on their lead singer, so I guess it's not such a bad thing."

"If I came across as a creep though, Bea, I'm sorry."

"No, you really haven't Aaron. Honestly, it's fine." I replied sincerely, "It's actually pretty nice to be thought of so highly. I love my job so much but it's made even better when I get positive feedback and of course, how often does a girl go on tour with her favourite band?"

"Not often, I guess. So I haven't put you off the tour then?"

"What? No way," I replied, secretly wanting to just jump on him and have my wicked way, but who would look like the weirdo then? I couldn't remember the last time someone had walked me to the door. It may not have been my house, granted, but the sentiment was still the same.

Aaron fumbled in his pocket for his key and clearly struggled to open the door of the band's large, detached, six bedroom house.

"It's Jim's," Aaron said, almost preempting my impending question, "we all live so far apart these days so this place makes a lot of sense. It's ours whilst we're being managed by Jim. It's our base." He swung the front door open and gestured for me to enter the house.

"After you, Beatrice."

"Why thank you, kind Sir." I replied, wondering if Aaron picked up on the flirty edge to my voice.

"No, thank you, Miss. The pleasure really is all mine!"

"Fancy a night cap?" Aaron shouted from the Victorian style kitchen, just after he'd given me the grand tour.

"Why not; I suppose one more drink won't hurt," I replied, knowing full well that actually, yes it would. *Oh well, when in Rome*, I thought. "What do you have?"

"Um, what don't we have?" Aaron replied, laughing, "There's wine; red and white, Remy, Jack Daniels. Or if you prefer, you can just have a hot drink?"

"No way," I called back, "hot drinks are for losers! I'll have a Remy please." I could already taste the first sip of brandy sliding down my throat.

"Coming right up."

After a few minutes, Aaron shuffled into the room with two huge fishbowl glasses with definitely more than a double measure in each.

"Wow. There's enough in here to last me into next week, let alone tonight. I thought it was just going to be a night cap?" I said, wondering how on earth I was going to drink it all.

"That's one thing you'll learn about me, Bea; I

don't do anything by half!"

The only time I'd ever heard Aaron Holmes speak was in between songs at the many Shout the Call gigs I'd been to and the odd television and radio interview and most recently, on our walk back from the pub but, as we sat drinking our brandy and chatting away, I was lulled by his shy, sweet, London accent. His bravado had all but disappeared and he seemed a different man now that we were on our own.

I sat across from him in an armchair that felt like one huge hug and knew that if I sank any deeper into its tartan fabric embrace, I would be asleep.

"Bea, why don't you come sit next to me?" Aaron asked, almost sensing my lethargy. Oh man, it was happening. I was going to get close to him; closer than any fan had probably dared to dream of. It probably wasn't even a good idea but how could I refuse such an offer.

"I'm okay thanks, Aaron."

"It's pretty obvious you're not," Aaron replied, "every time you look like you're just about to settle, you start fidgeting. Anyway, I'd like for you to sit over here." He patted the cushion to the right of him on the matching tartan sofa.

I heaved myself up from the armchair, picked up my fish bowl and walked around the coffee table to Aaron's side. I sat a comfortable distance away. As much as I wanted to get closer to him, in many more ways than one, I also wanted to remain professional. I was here to do a job, after all.

"I don't bite you know," Aaron said, looking directly at me – a suggestive smirk playing on his lips.

"Oh really; that's a shame!" I replied shakily. What the hell was I doing? Was it the brandy making me feel hot?

"Come on, Bea; come here," Aaron said, laughing, outstretching his right hand to me.

I scooted nervously up next to him. I had *never ever* been so forward with anyone of the opposite sex like this. I don't know what had got into me. I mentally scolded myself for being so, as my Nan used to say, *loose*. I knew drinking all day was a stupid idea. Aaron picked up his glass and sipped at his brandy, giving me *that* smirk. Did he know it was driving me wild? This time though, there was a 'far-away' look in his eyes.

"Penny for them?" I asked. It seemed we both had a lot on our minds.

"What? Oh, nothing," he replied before taking another sip of his drink.

"Oh okay, it's just you seem a little preoccupied," I

replied awkwardly.

"Yes, maybe I am," he said, turning full on to look at me, "I like you, Bea, I really like you."

Panic. Breathe. Calm. Panic.

"I like you too, Aaron."

"No. I mean I really like you," he replied, gulping nervously, "a lot."

"Don't be silly. We've only just met." I said and immediately regretted the statement. I didn't mean for it to sound so brash especially seeing as I actually felt the same.

"Why should that matter?" Aaron asked as his face moved a fraction of an inch closer to mine. I gulped and let out a shaky breath - now Aaron knew he'd got to me.

"It just does" I replied, knowing full well that it really didn't. "I'm here to do a job and I have to do it well. This is a big thing for me, and the company, more importantly. I cannot screw this up."

"Fuck the company for a second," Aaron shot at me before swilling back the remainder of his brandy in one fell swoop, "Bea – don't tell me you can't feel this? There's something between us; we have some kind of spark. You feel that, don't you?"

I couldn't disagree. He was right. I did feel something almost electric between us and it was exciting but at the same time, it was all a little too intense. I didn't know him, not really. My heart was screaming at me to tell him, *yes, I feel it too* but my head had put the hazard lights on.

"What's the worst that could happen?" Aaron continued. He stroked down my left arm and those blue-green eyes looked deep into mine.

"Oh wait, let me see," I replied, hoping the goose bumps his touch had left behind, wouldn't show, "I could lose my job!"

"What? Don't be ridiculous, Bea! You're honestly telling me your boss actually gives a shit about stuff like that? He's only interested in you doing your job and doing it right. What you do in your own time has nothing to do with him."

And then we were silent, deep in our own thoughts. Would it be so bad to just let myself go with him? Like he said, as long as I did my job properly, would it really bother Hanley and the company what I got up to on a personal level?

Aaron leaned in even closer to me and it was his whole body this time, not just his face. My inhibitions disappeared as I instinctively followed suit, letting my eyes close. I felt almost scared about what was about to happen.

I had had dream after dream about kissing Aaron Holmes. The dreams were always amazing. The reality, however, completely blew my mind.

Chapter 4

Aaron pulled out of the kiss, leaving me pouting into thin air with my eyes closed.

"Hhmmmm," he sighed, "that was nice."

"Huh? Um, yes," I agreed dreamily, "it was wasn't it?"

"You okay, Bea?"

"I think so."

"Okay," he said, drawing the word out, "So are we still cool?" Aaron asked.

"Of course, but I just want you to know that I don't usually do this Aaron," I said, trying to justify my actions,

"I barely know you but at the same time it doesn't feel *weird* at all."

"Well if I've overstepped the mark, Bea, I'm sorry. It just felt right."

"Look," I replied, "if it didn't feel right, I wouldn't have kissed you back.

Aaron nodded and smiled sweetly.

"Hey, would you like another brandy?"

"You know what, I think I will. It will probably calm me down a bit before bed."

I daydream, a lot, and as soon as Aaron left the living room to go through to the kitchen my mind was awash with a myriad of thoughts and feelings.

I had to be just about the luckiest girl alive. It was obvious that he liked me but then I suppose he did this kind of thing with lots of other girls on every tour. I'm sure I wasn't the first and I had a very strong feeling that I definitely wouldn't be the last.

Hanley told me to enjoy myself and that's all I could do. My thoughts swiftly conjured up an altogether different and more enjoyable image next. It was more than easy to imagine how fit Aaron would look underneath his casual, yet stylish indie clothes. I imagined him leaning over me with that wild mane of locks tickling my face, then my neck and then...

"Here you go," Aaron spoke, quickly causing the pictures in my head to dissipate, "we might as well finish the bottle huh?"

I nodded in agreement. It definitely wasn't the best idea but I didn't stop him from pouring even more liquor into my glass.

"Are you sure that's it now?" I said letting out a nervous giggle, "because if you ply me with any more alcohol, you might have to carry me to bed." I laughed nervously realising how suggestive that sounded.

"Okay," Aaron replied with a grin, "drink up then!"

******

It was ten thirty am. This annoyed me – I never sleep in, especially not until this time. I woke to find Aaron asleep on the thickly carpeted floor, a blanket covering his modesty. His breathing was soft and steady. His lips were parted very slightly. He looked as good, if not better, than when he was awake. I expected to find him in bed next to me, but it seems Aaron was as much a gentleman as he was a terrible flirt. It would have been so easy for us to let *things* happen last night and I was sure that *things* would have happened but it was refreshing and somewhat surprising that, for whatever reason, we had decided to sleep alone.

I slowly inched towards the edge of the bed. I had to get up; I needed to get my head together. Just when I thought I was successful in not waking the gorgeous creature lying there on the floor, it sat upright, rubbing sleep from its eyes.

"Where do you think you're going?" Aaron asked in a sexy, fresh-from-sleep drawl.

"Oh, hey," I replied, "How did you sleep?"

Aaron shook his head and tutted at me.

"Don't play that one on me. Don't avoid the question by asking another."

"Okay, okay," I replied, "you got me. I'm just a little nervous, that's all. I don't usually do this kind of thing."

"What kind of thing? We didn't *do it* if that's what you're thinking. We did stuff but we didn't do *that*, I promise."

"Well I guessed that when I realised you were asleep on the floor," I replied.

"Cool. So where's the problem?"

"Well, when you put it like that, there isn't one," I answered, "It's just that I don't want things to get complicated. I don't want either of us to get hurt."

"And why would that happen?"

"Aaron, you're the singer in a famous rock band. I know what kind of thing goes on, on tour. If we were to ever start getting serious, one or both of us will inevitably get hurt."

"Are you talking about *groupies*?" Aaron laughed. "Been there, done that and got the lipstick stained t-shirt. I'm past that now, Bea, seriously."

"You're honestly telling me that you don't *do* that kind of thing?" I asked, "I bet you've got fan-girls falling all over you."

"Of course I have and yes I did, a lot," he answered bluntly, "but I'm a big lad now. If I really wanted to take a fan up on a promise, I would but if I met the *right* person, well – everything changes then. And anyway, it all depends what you're up for - a bit of fun or a meaningful relationship."

I didn't know what to say. I mean, I have dreamt about being Aaron Holmes' girlfriend so many times. I have dreamt about being on tour with him – dreamt about being the woman he comes home to but this is now, and it's very, very real.

"I don't know what I'm *up for*," I began to answer, feeling my cheeks flush; talk about digging a hole, "I'm still coming to terms with the fact that all this is happening."

"Look, Bea, it's really very simple" Aaron said in all seriousness, "I really like you. You know that. What you don't know is that I'm a traditional kind of guy when it all boils down to it. I'm not a cheat and I don't set out to break hearts. Take from that what you will."

He paused for breath which allowed me a moment to process what he was telling me.

"This is not something I do very often either, you know - tell a girl how I feel about her – how I really feel. It's never been like that; there's never been a need. It's just been meaningless sex. You wouldn't believe how soul destroying that is."

His voice cracked on the last word and he shook his head.

"You feel a sense of euphoric release for a few moments and then it's over. I was always chasing that feeling with lots of girls but it gets you down," he continued, "Bea, I asked for you specifically because I learnt about you. I read about you and if I'm being totally honest, I do have other motives for getting you on board. And now you're here and you're even more amazing in person.

So, that's how I feel. I can't be any more honest with you. More than anything, I want a constant companion – someone to come home to. I need that now."

Maybe that's exactly what I needed too.

Chapter 5

We spent the rest of the day just chilling out, watching films and drinking red wine. The rest of the band were minding their own and pottering around through the house.

"One more bottle?" Aaron asked, tipping the bottle upside down and tapping its base.

"We really shouldn't," I replied.

"Why?"

"Oh, well since you're twisting my arm," I answered, smiling – that didn't need much persuasion "At least I'll be preparing my body for the next few weeks or so."

We both laughed.

"Yup," Aaron said, feigning seriousness, "We do like a drink or two and we do love to party. Any designs you have on having your full quota of eight hours sleep a night should be scrapped. Seriously, I can't remember the last time I really slept; well at least not properly, anyway."

This wasn't the best of news. If I don't eat and sleep well I get angry and irritable. I'm sure Shout the Call had no problems living that way. I suppose when they're out doing what they do, adrenaline kicks in and somehow, they manage to get by. Whether I would was another matter entirely.

"You want to come down to the cellar?" Aaron asked, "It's my favourite place in the entire house and not just because it's where I keep the wine I've collected from all over the world..."

Aaron stopped for a second and looked almost apologetic for bragging.

"The acoustics are awesome," he went on, "It's where I spend practically all of my time. It's just a very special place and it's where I feel most at peace. It's also where I write about ninety percent of our songs. Come down with me, I think you'll love it."

Aaron got up from the settee, gave me his hand, pulled me up and led me through to the kitchen before opening a door that presented a stone stairway, leading down to the cellar. Aaron took me through, flicked on a wall light and shut the door behind him. As we came to about half way down, I was taken aback by the room before me. I could totally see and feel why Aaron loved it down here so much.

******

This was no cellar – it was a bloody bungalow! In the far corner of the room was a cozy living area that had a sofa-bed, a coffee table, a small dining table, cupboards, and a fridge. This all took up at least half of the cellar. The other half was part recording studio – part wine cellar. If Aaron wasn't careful, he would wind up living down here without the need to see or speak to the rest of the band.

"So, you like it?" Aaron asked nervously.

"Um, yeah!" I answered eagerly, "it's amazing."

"You know, I'm not a recluse or anything," Aaron went on, "it's just that I like to have my own space. You won't believe this but I'm not the drugged- up alcoholic the press would have you believe."

"Aaron, I'm the last person to believe the drivel that the national press prints," I assured him, "I used to work for my local newspaper and left within months of starting there. I walked out because I refused to print lies and that's all I'm going to say on that matter."

"Oh right, okay," Aaron replied, looking as though he knew he'd touched a nerve but he also looked thankful too.

"So anyway," he went on, "shall we just stay down here? I was only going to have one more drink, if you're up for it."

"One more then and that's it, okay?"

"Cool," Aaron replied excitedly as he pulled a bottle out from the wall; a whole wall that was one huge wine rack. Amazing really wasn't the word.

******

It was nearing four pm and I was starting to feel anxious. At six thirty, we would be getting on the tour bus to Dover and heading to Calais. This sounds pretty pathetic but the furthest I had ever been from home, up until now, was the Isle of Arran in Scotland. I had always dreamt of travelling far further afield but my measly budget wouldn't allow that. New Music; Non Stop changed all that in such a short amount of time. I mean, eighteen months is no time at all in the grand scheme of things.

"Aaron, where the bloody hell are ya?" I heard Jim shout from upstairs.

Aaron kept still and silent and gestured for me to follow suit. His shoulders began to shake and I could tell straight away that he was giggling, albeit very quietly.

"Aaron!" Jim yelled again, "For crying out loud, mate, get up here now and get your shit together. Have you seen the time?"

I wanted to open my mouth to answer. I know how Jim must have been feeling. I'm all for a good time but when there are deadlines to adhere to, a line has to be drawn. I wanted to call back but before a word could escape my mouth, Aaron pressed his to mine, silencing me with his heavenly lips. I melted into the kiss immediately and time suddenly meant nothing.

I couldn't believe what was happening and how his kiss was making me feel. Aaron, it seemed, was more than aware of how this particular practical joke was affecting me.

"Sod ya then," Jim shouted once more, "I've had enough of your bullshit!"

Aaron broke off the kiss and fell about giggling. I

didn't laugh along with him. He took me by surprise and although I enjoyed our off-the-cuff clinch, I was flabbergasted by what had just happened.

"Are you okay?" he whispered.

"I guess so."

Aaron looked concerned. He was obviously wondering whether he had overstepped the mark by kissing me out of the blue but he seemed confused too – I didn't exactly help matters by being as much into the kiss as he was. I couldn't stop the sigh of relief coming from my mouth as Aaron opened the cellar door to the kitchen.

"Jim, have you been after me?" he asked.

"Bloody hell, Aaron!" Jim shot back, "We need to pack up and get out. Think you can cope?"

"I'm sure I'll be fine," Aaron answered nonchalantly, "I have Bea here to help me if I get into any bother."

Jim looked straight at me, annoyed.

"I'm sorry Jim," I shot out before Aaron had chance to shut me up; "It's my fault. I asked Aaron if he could take me down the cellar…."

"You wouldn't believe how very wrong but so very right that sounds." Aaron said, laughing at the innuendo in my apology.

"Enough. I really don't need to know what you pair have been up to," Jim said, waving his hands in our face as if trying to swat away his imagination like a fly.

"Really Jim," I went on, trying not to let embarrassment get the better of me, "It really is not what you think."

"Bea, love; I don't give two hoots what you do or don't do with Aaron or any of the other band members, for that matter," Jim said plainly, "as long as you do what you're being paid to, that's fine with me. The way you conduct yourself outside of the business part of this, well, it's your call."

Jim smiled at me, a fatherly smile. He knew I was getting worked up. I smiled back nervously.

"Anyway, we've just wasted precious time having this conversation," Jim said, glancing at his watch. "Now get off with ya. Get yourself sorted, Aaron."

******

We made the ferry with minutes to spare. It seemed that Aaron had already packed the lion's share of his stuff, leaving just a few last minute bits and pieces to take care of. Jim seemed equally amazed and bewildered by the efficiency displayed by the band in getting ready.

Jim parked the tour bus up and checked we were all present as we piled out the door.

"Right, go and stretch your legs and grab a drink or two if you must, but please, let's not get trashed before we arrive in France," Jim warned, "We'll have plenty of time to make merry when we get there. Because we've travelled late, you've got tomorrow off but on Thursday, it all kicks off. Let's just take it easy eh?"

For the first time since Monday lunch time, the whole band seemed to agree.

A feeling of *déjà vu* coursed through me as we found a table big enough to accommodate the six of us. Liam Johnson, Shout the Call's lead guitarist, was the first to speak, not even waiting for our bums to touch the leatherette seats.

"So, what are we all having then? I'll get this one in."

"Bleedin' hell, that's a first!" scoffed Jack Illingsworth, the band's rhythm guitarist.

"Certainly is," Aaron agreed, "but if you're offering, JD for me please."

"Oooh, hitting the Bourbon like a boss already eh?"

Liam asked.

"Be rude not to," Aaron answered.

One by one, the rest of the band put their orders in and Jim shouted, "I'll have a shandy!" from the other side of the room.

"What you having, Bea?" Liam asked. Could I handle any more alcohol? I could imagine my little liver pleading with me; begging me not to let even one more drop of alcohol pass my lips.

"Just a mineral water for me please – still," I replied, knowing what the reaction would be.

"No chance," Liam shot back, "Look here, lady - you're on tour with Shout the Call now, not a bunch of nuns. Let your hair down and go crazy!"

I sighed in deep realisation. I suppose if you can't beat them, you may as well join them.

Chapter 6

A few hours and two glasses of red wine later, we were all back on the bus, sat round the dining table. We weren't moving anywhere as we waited in the queue to leave the ferry. We all chatted but Aaron was unusually quiet, he almost seemed uncomfortable.

"Everything okay?" I whispered, turning to face him.

"What?" Aaron answered slowly. He definitely wasn't *'in the room'*, "Oh um, yes, I'm fine."

I'm no body language expert, that's for sure, but it was blindingly obvious Aaron was far from fine. I put my left hand on his right knee and felt his muscles tighten and flinch at the contact. He was so on edge.

Something was unnerving about how he was acting but I couldn't quite put my finger on what. His hands were fidgeting on the table so I gathered all my courage and pulled him up out of his seat, not even bothering to apologise to the guys as I whisked him away. Aaron dragged behind like a lost puppy; he put up no resistance in being taken away from his gang. I spun him round so we faced each other, put both my hands on his shoulders and gently forced him to sit down on his bunk. His head hung low. I stood in front of him, wondering if I could seek out any kind of explanation for his peculiar behaviour. Nothing was forthcoming.

"You're really not okay, are you?" I asked.

No answer.

"Aaron, come on – you can talk to me. Something's upset you, hasn't it?" I asked again.

Aaron snorted a strained chuckle and shook his head in reply.

"Well what is it then? Have I done something to upset you?"

Aaron laughed again and this time there was something strangely sinister about its tone. I didn't like it one little bit.

"Aaron, stop it! You're starting to worry me."

"*Worry* you?" Aaron said, confused.

"Yes."

"Why?"

"I don't know," I replied, calming very slightly now he was actually responding, "you're just acting really weird."

He laughed again, and again I couldn't see what he found so funny. If I wasn't being paid to be on the tour with this bloody band, I would have got my stuff and got the hell out. Aaron looked straight into my eyes, turning suddenly serious.

"It's not you, Bea."

"Well that's good but it still doesn't explain anything though, does it?"

"What needs to be explained exactly?" Aaron asked.

I looked at him blankly, shaking my head. If I couldn't make him see how ridiculously he was behaving, what was the point? Aaron looked away from me, shrugging his shoulders.

"Please tell me what's going on, Aaron. This is ridiculous."

Aaron looked straight at me again. His eyes bored

into mine and I immediately felt vulnerable.

"All you need to know is that it's not you, Bea," Aaron answered, his voice trembling. Was he starting to get upset?

"So you've said," I said, calmly this time, "but why don't I believe you?"

"I mean it – you have done absolutely nothing wrong. I really, really, like you Bea. I can't tell you that enough. You're beautiful, funny, sweet, caring, amazing – shit, I can't think of any more glowing adjectives. You're just perfect."

I felt like I had been hit by a ton of bricks. I knew Aaron liked me but not as much as that. The second I started to warm to him again, I snapped back to defence mode.

"But?" I asked.

"Yup, there's always a 'but' isn't there, honey?"

"Well, actually – no, there isn't always, Aaron," I answered, "You know, sometimes two people can connect and just enjoy each other's company. Why has it all got to be so complicated?" I shook my head in total frustration. How the tables turn. Yesterday we were having pretty much the exact same conversation except that it was me being the weird, over-analytical one.

"I'm sorry, Bea, I really am. I will talk to you about this, I promise. I'll tell you everything when it feels right. That's all I can say right now. Do you trust me?"

Now that was a good question. If it had been anyone else, any other man, the answer would have been an emphatic *no* but something deep inside told me I could.

"Yes. I do."

Chapter 7

I woke up feeling pretty fresh. Considering how much alcohol I had consumed the night before, I was expecting to feel like death. I was also expecting a bit of an atmosphere between me and Aaron. He knew that I knew he was holding something back. But it could all wait, at least just for the time being because we were in Paris and I wanted to make the very most of my day off in a place I had always wanted to visit.

Washing, changing and generally getting ready is normally easy enough but it's a different story altogether when you're trying to tip-toe around the bodies of crashed out band members who had decided there wasn't much point in actually going to bed. I chuckled to myself as I cast my eyes over them all, splayed out on any surface that looked comfortable enough to lie down on. The snoring almost sounded harmonious.

Happy that I was finally done and ready to go, I pressed the button beside the bus door and it slid open automatically.

"Christ, Jim," I said, startled.

"Alright, Bea," he smiled, "You're a bit jumpy ain't ya?"

"No, I'm fine," I lied, wondering if he could see through it, "It's just a case of too much alcohol and not enough sleep I think. I'm completely out of my league with this lot!"

"Right," Jim said before chuckling kindly, "you don't really seem the type that could match these guys when it comes to burning the candle at both ends; no offence."

I laughed.

"No offence taken, Jim; I really don't know how they do it. I just can't wait to start work properly. At least it will give me a breather."

"You do realise that you'll be expected at *every* after-show party, right?"

"Seriously?"

"Completely," Jim answered, "are you sure you're

okay though, chuck. No one been upsetting you have they?"

"Nope; everything's cool."

"Well, look, Bea, if you have any issues with the work in hand or indeed, any of these bloody gadabouts, you just come and talk to me, right?"

For some stupid reason, I felt my throat go tight with emotion. I trusted Jim and I knew he meant every word of what he said. I wanted to tell him everything that had happened between me and Aaron, obviously omitting certain details, but if I was being honest, what was there to '*tell*'? I couldn't tell Jim something I didn't fully understand in the first place.

"Aw, thanks, Jim," I replied, urging my voice not to wobble, "that means a lot to me. Thank you."

"My pleasure, chuck," Jim said, giving me a kind wink.

******

There wasn't enough time to see all the sights because I had to be ready and available to shoot when the band was set to sound-check at six pm, so my day was spent sitting outside coffee shops, drinking some of the best coffee I have ever tasted and when I found a *boulangerie, patisserie* and *delicatessen* within yards of each other, I splurged on cheese, olives and fresh, crusty baguettes and more than a few sweet treats to take back to the bus for us all to enjoy. I was loaded with bags and had far too much coffee in my system (probably for the best) and as I charged through the door, there was only one face to meet mine.

"Hey, you," Aaron said, catching me and stopping me from falling flat on my face.

"Hey," I replied breathlessly, looking past him, into the bus to see who may have witnessed my embarrassing little trip. Thankfully the bus empty, "where are the guys?"

"Oh, they shot off for sound-check," Aaron answered.

"But it's only five twenty. They're eager aren't they?"

"Well, I actually asked them to go a bit earlier," Aaron answered, looking sheepishly pale.

"Oh, okay?" I trailed off.

"I just told them that we, you and me, had things to discuss and off they went without a word. I think they guessed something was wrong last night."

"Yes, well it's all sorted now isn't it?" I asked, as much to myself as well as Aaron.

"Yeah but I do really need to talk to you. There's something you really ought to know."

Once again, Aaron was starting to worry me.

"About?" I asked, unsure whether I really wanted to know.

"Oh shit, Bea," Aaron said nervously, letting out a long, heavy sigh, "This is going to be hard and you'll never believe me but, well, it's true. Believe what you want." He took my hand and led me to over to the settee.

"Sit down, please," he said.

I did as I was told. Aaron took a deep breath and exhaled. It seemed this was going to be one hell of a chat. As he opened his mouth to speak, the bus door flew open.

"Thank God!" Jim shouted, looking shook up, "sorry to disturb you guys but Aaron, you need to come with me – *now!*"

"What? Can't it wait?" Aaron asked as he dropped my limp, clammy hand.

"No. Not at all," Jim answered, "just hurry!"

Chapter 8

I chased after Aaron but was swiftly pulled back, halfway between the bus and the venue, by an ashen faced Jim.

"No, Bea," he said, almost completely out of breath, "this is something you need to keep out of and I mean that in the nicest possible way."

I shook my head in confusion; what the hell was going on?

"Okay, Jim," I replied, feigning trust. There was no way I was about to brush any of this under the table.

Jim rubbed my arm and looked at me apologetically before dashing off.

******

At seven pm I was ushered from the bus to our room backstage which had a fridge full of beer, a basic but clean washroom and toilet, four three seat settees and tea and coffee making facilities. It was far better than I was expecting. At eight fifteen the support band (a local group I had never heard of but who sounded amazing) played the last song of their set. I grew increasingly nervous as I watched Shout the Call chewing their nails and drumming their fingers in anticipation. Aaron paced back and forth like a caged animal. It was hard to see him so wound up but at the same time I could easily understand how anxious he and the rest of the band were. I walked up to him and softly stroked his arms.

"Aaron," I said, trying to push my own nervousness to the back of my mind, "you keep pacing like that and there won't be any floor left."

"Oh yeah," he said, emitting a feeble laugh, "Sorry, honey."

"Hey, I'm only kidding," I said, rubbing his shoulders, "I can't imagine how nerve wracking it must be to play to so many people but I *can* imagine how amazing it must be. They're all here for you."

"What do you mean, *here for you?*" Aaron asked, immediately jumping on the defence.

"Well, you know – everyone in that crowd is here for you. You can't tell me that the crowd, especially the girls, don't hang off every single word you sing and say?"

"Doesn't bother me to be honest."

"What?" I scoffed, noticing Aaron's face turn serious again, almost angry, "you can't tell me that you don't love the attention?"

"Might do but then again, I might not!" he shot back sharply.

"Bloody hell, Aaron," I retaliated; there was no way he was getting off with talking to me like that!

What on earth was wrong with him? It felt like I was walking on egg shells around him. I had to just wing it and hope for the best, "I was just saying, that's all. You're in this well known band and you have thousands upon thousands of fans. You've got to get a high off seeing so many people, night after night. It's got to give you a buzz."

"I guess you're right, Bea," he said, "it just sounded like you were implying I only do it for the attention."

"No, not at all; if that's how it sounded, then I'm sorry. I really didn't mean it that way."

"I'm sorry, Bea, it's just the nerves kicking in. No matter how many times I do this, it never gets easier. You'd think I would know how to cope with it but, well –

you can see I don't. I'm sorry for being such a dick. I don't want to upset you – I just want you to believe that. "

I felt my throat tighten, which usually meant I was on the verge of tears. I turned away from him, took a deep breath and turned back round, composure somewhat restored.

He seemed to sense the atmosphere between us and as much as I wanted to, I could not resist the hug he pulled me into. In fact, I sank into it, taking in his scent and strength; finding solace in his embrace and just as I was settling in nicely, he gently pushed me away and out of his arms.

"Bea, I promise you this, I really, really like you," he said, "I just hope you can see past the ego and like me too."

He looked at me expectantly, hoping for some kind of response.

"Oh Aaron," I replied, "I really like you too but then I think you already know that."

"Shall we just push aside my little diva-fit and enjoy the evening?"

"That sounds like a plan," I said. We both let out long sighs of relief as if we had been holding our breath since we began our little *tiff*.

"But, Aaron," I went on, "I know there's something you're not telling me and at some point, I need to know what's going on. We just need to be honest with each other, okay?"

He nodded and pulled me into his arms. He kissed my forehead and I melted.

******

I took my place in the pit and readied myself for shooting Shout the Call for the very first time and although I felt like I had lived a mini lifetime with Aaron and the band already, I was excited; seriously excited. At nine pm, the room went black and even with my ear plugs in, the sound of the crowd whooping, hollering and screaming was almost ear splitting. *'Blitzkrieg Bop'* by The Ramones played over the PA and I immediately felt pumped. As far as I was aware, I was the only photographer allowed in the pit for the whole gig but I made a conscious decision I would stop shooting after four songs. I wanted to be in the thick of it, watching my favourite band of all time blow the crowd away.

The band suddenly filed on to stage and blasted out the opening riff of *'You Really Shouldn't'* and that was my cue to get the money shot. The second I pointed my camera up at Aaron, he flashed me a look that made me feel like I was the only girl in the room that mattered.

Without realising, I found myself at the bar. I had finished shooting and was thirsty, so I ordered a pint of cider and stood at the back of the room watching the crowd lap up the band, the music and the atmosphere. I'm no fool; it was more than easy to see why all the girls, and a fair few of the men, idolised Aaron. I could see it because I felt exactly the same as them. Aaron was charismatic and captivating on stage. He had the crowd in the palm of his hand. Of course, the rest of the band was on fire too.

The gig flew by. I made my way backstage to prepare for my first Shout the Call interview. Jim stood, side of stage, waiting for me. He took my hand and gave me a paternal peck on the cheek.

"You ready for this, Bea?"

"Like you'll never believe," I replied, flashing him a warm smile.

******

Jim showed me through to our room and the sight of

table after table full of French delicacies made my mouth water and my stomach groan. The smell of fresh bread, garlic and cheese swamped my senses. Was this how the band were treated in every venue they played? Jim gasped. It seemed I wasn't the only one who was surprised by the spread that had been put out for us.

"Make yourself comfy then, Bea." Jim said as he reluctantly turned to head back out the door.

"Thanks, Jim. Are you not staying?"

"As much as I would love to, Bea," he replied, eyes scouting the room again, almost salivating, "someone's got to rally the troops."

"I'll go, Jim. I'll find them. You look tired."

"Blimey, thanks, Bea – you really know how to make a guy feel special."

I laughed and Jim's fake scowl turned in to a wide smile. He started to laugh too.

"Seriously though," I went on, patting him on the shoulder, "you've done so much already; driving and organising and whatnot. It's the least I can do. Have a little break eh?"

"That sounds a very good idea," Jim answered.

I turned past Jim, assuming he had taken me up on

the offer. As I grabbed the handle of the door though, Jim took hold of my wrist, stopping me in my tracks.

"No, Bea, honestly; you're better staying here, love."

******

It seemed silly of me not to take advantage of such generous hospitality so whilst I had some time alone I helped myself to some *Camembert* and crusty French bread. It was delicious. The profiteroles were beyond amazing; I had never tasted any this good before. I washed it all down with a large glass of *Cabernet Sauvignon*.

I waited for what felt like forever and it was getting a little tedious. I needed to go and stretch my legs just to rid myself of the boredom I was feeling. Of course, it had nothing to do with the fact that I was nosy and wanted to know why Jim didn't want me to go after the guys – *yeah, right!* Actually, all I really wanted to do was get the interview in the bag and then we could all go off and do whatever we wanted.

I peeped my head out from behind the door and scanned the corridor. All was clear and considering we were in a concert hall, the venue was eerily quiet. The band had been off stage for around an hour but as with any gig, you always get the stragglers and the *hardcore* fans hanging out, hoping to get photos, autographs and even talk to their heroes but it really was far too silent. I couldn't put my finger on exactly what but something didn't feel right. I headed down the corridor until I found myself standing right outside the stage door.

I took hold of its handle. Half of me berated myself for not taking Jim's advice; the last thing I wanted to do was upset him and lose his trust. The other half was telling me to get a grip and get on with it. I punted on the latter and hoped for the best.

I took a long, deep breath and grabbed the handle; I pulled it down and pushed the door wide open. I couldn't stop the scream that erupted from mouth.

Chapter 9

My feet were rooted to the spot. I wanted to run but it was impossible; my body obviously wasn't receiving the signals my brain was screaming at it. The scene before me disgusted me but at the same time, I was fascinated. Aaron turned around and looked straight at me. His hands and mouth were covered in the blood of the girl that had just slumped to the floor behind him. His eyes were glimmering like pools of bright aqua and he looked incredible; more gorgeous than I had ever seen him before. I hated myself for even thinking that. How messed up; how could I even think that? How could I see past the horror?

He walked towards me and I was completely mesmerised. I couldn't take my eyes off him, which was a blessing in disguise given the fact that all I could hear was the chomping and slobbering as the rest of the band continued on with their feast regardless. Bile rose up from my stomach and I turned to wretch. I felt Aaron's hand brush down my arm.

"Bea, I can explain….."

"Oh really," I shouted.

"I know how this must look and I can understand how scared you must be."

"How this must look? How scared I must be?" I said, my voice cracking with anger, "This should be scaring me, Aaron but the awful thing is that I'm not terrified and that terrifies me. I can't see past you and how you make me feel. I'm disgusted at myself more than I am of you. It's all so wrong."

"It's because you love me."

"Excuse me?" I barked in utter disbelief. Could he have got any further up his own arse?

"Don't deny it, Bea. Love is blindness."

I was truly lost for words because Aaron was completely right even though I hadn't told him how I really felt about him, how I was hopelessly in love with him. My blinkered, dream like vision was getting in the way of rational thought.

"Get lost, Aaron!" I shouted angrily, "How can you say that after what you've done?"

"I love you, Bea; please let me explain."

I stared blankly at him. Tonight was definitely a night for shocks and surprises. I could hear the words coming from his perfect mouth but I couldn't absorb them. Did he just say he *loves* me?

"I know this must all be so scary for you, Bea; it would scare anyone I guess," he went on.

"You guess?" I asked sarcastically then nodded, "yes, you guess right."

I shook my head, hoping it would clear it.

"I don't know why I'm still here, Aaron; still talking to you. I should report this to the police. I should let people know what you are; what you all are! I should also get my shit together and get out of here."

"But you're not going to, are you, Bea? I won't stop you from going because I love you but I know you don't really want to leave." Aaron shook his head and sighed, "I know this must sound ridiculous but please understand. Can we talk about this somewhere else; somewhere more private?"

"I think we've talked enough, don't you?"

"No, actually" Aaron replied as he wiped his bloodied mouth on his toned right arm, "you don't know the half of it."

******

Aaron didn't seem to care that we were sat in a coffee shop, of all places, talking about his life as a vampire. Considering the sign on the door suggested it was '*open twenty four hours*', the shop was, excuse the pun, *dead*.

"I wanted to tell you the moment you joined us," Aaron said slowly, the words reluctant to leave his mouth, "but just when I think the moment is right, we get interrupted."

"So that's your excuse and you're sticking to it, right?"

"No, not an excuse, Bea; the truth," Aaron answered, "believe what you want. This isn't something you can just casually drop into conversation."

He had a point.

"No shit, Sherlock. Aaron, I am so at odds with

myself you would not believe. It's all so wrong and messed up."

"If I were in your shoes, I'm sure I'd feel the same," Aaron went on, clearly stating the obvious *again*, "but love does that kind of thing to you. You think I could do to you what I did to that girl? Bea, I really care about you."

I wanted to scream at him; I wanted to tell him how full of himself he was but I just couldn't find the words to do it.

"I still don't understand," I said, trying desperately to get things straight in my head, "are you saying you can't hurt me because you love me? How can I trust you on that? You're a vampire for Christ's sake!"

"I promise I will never hurt you," Aaron replied.

"But my blood flows, Aaron, the same as anybody else. You can't guarantee you won't feed on me?"

"Well, no, I can't guarantee anything but if I feel it might get to that point, I will leave; I won't come near you ever again. I won't ever let it get that far, Bea, please just trust me on that."

"I guess I'll just have to take your word for it then," I said because, after all, what else could I do?

******

"Good morning, you two," Jim greeted us as he opened the tour bus door, "do you know what time it is?"

I looked at my watch and was shocked to see it was just past two thirty in the morning. Aaron and I got to the coffee shop just before midnight. The time had flown.

"Sorry, Jim," I whispered, caffeine drunk, "did we wake you?"

"No, sweet," Jim answered, "one thing you'll come to learn about me is I'll only rest when all the flock has returned, which now includes you."

"Thanks, Jim," I said as I went up on tip toes and kissed his cheek. I took a quick glance around the bus and saw that only we were back, "Looks like you'll be awake a while longer then."

"Yes, the joys of being a manager eh?"

Aaron went straight to the fridge and pulled out a beer.

"Jim? Bea?" he turned and asked as Jim and I crashed out on the settee, "beer?"

"I'll have a Jack actually mate," Jim replied instantly, "I need something a bit stronger tonight, or should I say this morning."

Aaron looked at me with a smile, silently asking me

again. For a moment, I plunged head first into those aqua blue eyes. Once again, I was hypnotised.

"Bea, earth calling Bea; do you want a beer?"

"Um, no thanks," I stuttered, "actually, do we have any brandy?"

"Coming right up."

I was starting to come down from the coffee and tiredness was setting in; a brandy was exactly the tonic to knock me out for the night.

"Is everything okay, Bea?" Jim asked me but glared at Aaron.

"Jim, she knows okay," Aaron answered for me, "Bea knows what we are."

"What the hell!" Jim said, looking bewildered.

"Jim, it's all my fault," I interrupted, "You tried to warn me. You told me to stay in hospitality; I didn't."

Jim's face turned white.

"Oh, Bea," he said, scooting around to sit beside me, "oh, darlin', are you okay?"

"Jim," I answered, patting his knee, "I'm fine. I think. Don't get me wrong, I'm not exactly jumping for joy, but well, that's all I can say right now. Anyway, where's that brandy?"

Aaron handed me a large, fishbowl glass full of the rich amber liquid.

I cupped the glass, swirling the brandy round before taking a slow, savouring sip.

"Good?" Aaron asked.

"Mmm," I sighed; eyes closed.

Aaron joined us, sitting on the settee opposite. We sat in silence for a while. It had been an eventful day to say the least and we all needed to wind down, if only for a short while.

"Well, don't I feel like the gooseberry?" Jim said awkwardly, before throwing back the rest of his Jack Daniels in one gulp and wincing, "Look, I'm off. I'm going to try and find the lads. I'll see you two early morning lovebirds in a bit." He grabbed his jacket off the back of the driver's seat and headed out.

"You want another?" Aaron asked me as he chugged back his own beer.

I nodded as I downed the rest of my brandy, something I never usually do. Aaron took my glass from me and poured another generous helping. I glanced at my watch and even though I felt truly exhausted, I didn't feel like I could sleep.

"Here you go," he said, handing the glass back to me. I made to take it from him but froze as our hands touched. It felt like electricity was flowing between the two of us. I couldn't pull my hand away as his eyes found mine. He didn't even have to open his beautiful mouth to render me speechless; he didn't have to do anything physical to immobilise me. It was all so exciting and actually, a little scary too.

"Shall we retire to my bunk?" he asked me, ripping me from my trance.

"As opposed to this luxurious, corner group settee?" I answered, laughing giddily.

Aaron laughed too and took our drinks to his bunk, putting them on the shelf at the foot of it. He sauntered back towards me and grabbed my hand, pulling me towards his bed.

"Do you want to, you know, talk some more about stuff?" he asked awkwardly, running his hand through his tousled, long, curly locks.

"That's the last thing I want right now," I replied as I grabbed Aaron's face and pulled him down on to me.

Chapter 10

The dynamic had changed between the two of us; I mean, how could it have not? I was filled with fear just knowing that his promise to not hurt me could be broken at any time and that meant I could lose him forever; something that could not happen. At the same time, I felt more excited than I'd ever been in my life.

Even though I had made a mental promise to myself to not give in, to not break my self-imposed *no-nookie* rule, I couldn't. It was impossible to resist when all I could feel was Aaron's chest pressed against my back, his arms wrapped around me protectively.

I had only ever dreamt of being with Aaron Holmes like this. Not once did I ever think it would happen. It blew all my dreamt-up expectations completely out of the water. Our lust was short lived though as he quickly pulled away from me covering his mouth to hide his fangs.

"Let me see, please?" I asked him as I gently pulled his hand away from his mouth.

Aaron didn't answer me but he put up no defense.

"Oh wow!"

"I'm sorry," he mumbled as he covered his mouth for the second time, "This cannot happen again."

"Oh, Aaron," I said, shaking my head, "Is it wrong for me to say I want it to? I didn't think you could look more amazing but you do. I know how ridiculously shallow that must sound."

"Um, no, not shallow; I'm just blown away that you're still here." Aaron said, uncovering his mouth again.

"Well I am," I said, "and I'm not going anywhere."

"I just couldn't help it, Bea; tonight feels different somehow."

"I know," I agreed, "that's exactly what I was thinking. It's so intense."

My brain went in to overdrive.

"I know what you are now," I continued, "What's the

point in trying to hide anything from me again. Are they still out?"

"These?" Aaron said smirking sexily, running his tongue over his still protruding canines.

******

"Blimey, good afternoon, you two," Jim said, looking up from his paper, "You have a good sleep?"

I nodded at Jim. It was all I could do to take the attention away from my cheeks that felt like they were turning every shade of red imaginable. Aaron was his usual cool, unflappable self. He ruffled his unruly bed hair.

"Hey, Jim," he yawned before looking at me sleepily.

"It's a bit late for breakfast, right, Bea?" he asked, a small smile breaking on his face; was he thinking about what happened last night? "What about we go and get lunch and coffee?"

"Sounds like a plan," I replied, mentally trying to decide upon an outfit.

I washed and changed quickly before Aaron had

chance to steal our tiny bathroom. I opted for a casual ensemble; black leggings, my over-sized lumberjack shirt and my beat up, worn out Converse. While Aaron was busy getting himself ready, I slumped down on the settee next to Jim. He looked at me with a knowing smile.

"What?" I asked.

"Nothing," he replied, smiling even wider.

I looked down at my hands and realised I was wringing them. *Get a grip,* I told myself, *how old are you again?* And then Aaron appeared in my peripheral vision. I turned round completely to take in the sight in front of me.

"You ready, Bea?" he asked.

"Um.." I said, hoping I had only imagined my jaw dropping open. "Oh, yes – sorry."

I stood up slowly and looked around to Jim. "See you later," I said blankly.

"Catch ya later, chuck; have a good 'un," Jim said, waving us off.

Aaron flashed a wink at Jim and pulled me outside. He slammed the door behind him.

"Take no notice of him, honey," Aaron said defensively, which struck me as odd, "he's just being nosy."

"Don't be silly," I replied, "I really like Jim; he reminds me a little of my dad."

"Right," he said before closing his hand tightly around mine. Public shows of affection were not usually my *thing*, no matter how small, but I didn't mind this one bit

We walked and walked until we practically stumbled upon a cobbled alleyway with a quaint little *café* at the end.

******

"Madam, Monsieur – please take a seat," the waiter greeted us, "What can I get for you?"

"*Merci beaucoup. Deux Americano café de se il vous plaît,*" Aaron said, surprising both me and the waiter.

"Certainly, Monsieur," our waiter replied, I'm sure only speaking English to help keep me abreast of the conversation, "Two café Americanos coming up. Would Sir and Madam like anything else?"

Aaron ordered cheese and biscuits for us both,

followed by chocolate tart. My mouth watered at the thought.

"An excellent choice, Sir and may I say, our chocolate tart is exquisite."

"*Merci encore,*" Aaron replied and I pretty much knew what that meant. Regardless of what Aaron had ordered, he sounded amazing and that's all I could compute.

"Wow. Someone really paid attention in French class, huh?" I said in awe, "I took French at school, but there's no way I would have sounded that good."

"Thanks," he said quietly, almost a little embarrassed, "And I'm sure you would sound great if you at least tried"

"No, believe me, you wouldn't be impressed. It sounds like it's your second language. You sound very comfortable."

"I suppose it comes with the territory really."

"How do you mean?" I asked as the waiter came back, placing our coffees on the table. Aaron smiled and nodded at him and waited for him to get out of earshot.

"Well, for your information, I did learn French at school – you're right, but it was way back in 1897 though."

"You were born in 1897?" I asked, dumbfounded.

"No, that's when I started to learn the language; I was eleven. Which means," he said smiling, pausing for dramatic effect and allowing me to try and get my head around what he was imparting, "I was born in 1886. I am 127 years old. Don't tell me; I'm looking good right?"

I couldn't answer him, not straight away. I had read the books and watched all the films where the vampires always seemed to be about a thousand years old or something, but this was real.

"Actually, you're looking more than good," I replied, "you look so good that you barely look a day over twenty one," I gushed, immediately feeling embarrassed for sounding so cheesy.

"Aww, thanks, honey" Aaron replied as he leant over the table, planting a kiss on my slightly open mouth. "I died when I was 27; it was 1913."

"How did you die?" I asked, feeling a deep sense of sadness fill my chest.

"I contracted smallpox, which was rife at the time, and before it went too far and killed me, I found a man that could help."

"Help?"

"Yes," Aaron nodded, "Bea, smallpox was a horrible disease. Good friends and members of my family contracted it too, before me - not one of them survived. The moment I started with the fever and the symptoms, I was offered a way out."

"So, this *man* offered it to you?"

"Yes."

"What happened?"

"He asked me if I wanted to live forever."

"And you did, obviously."

"Who wouldn't, Bea? I was too young to die. Death scared me and I just wasn't about to give up without a fight."

I was listening so intently to Aaron that it felt like there was absolutely no one else in the *café*.

"I wanted to see the world, Bea," Aaron continued, "and I craved knowledge. I needed to learn everything I could possibly learn. To do that, I could not meet the same fate that had met so many others. That's where James, or as you know him, Jim, came in."

"Jim?" I asked, once again, totally flabbergasted. The waiter came towards us with our food and Aaron quieted me, stopping whatever I was going to say next by putting his finger to my lips.

"*Jouir*; enjoy," the waiter exclaimed as he placed a slate slab in the middle of us, full of biscuits, cheeses and grapes.

Aaron nodded, itching to get back to his story.

"All clear," I whispered as the waiter disappeared from view.

"So, James 'Jim' Edwards is the wonderful man that turned me," Aaron went on, "He offered me an alternative; the best possible one."

"Without sounding completely stupid, I guess that means he bit you, right?" I asked, feeling just as I had said – completely stupid.

"That's correct. He almost drained me before allowing me to take on his blood and that, as they say, is history."

"Did it hurt?" I asked, "Can you even remember that far back?"

"Actually, it feels like it just happened yesterday, Bea. Did it hurt? Well, it wasn't particularly comfortable but once Jim had punctured skin and took first blood, the whole time he was feeding on me felt euphoric. I felt as close to what I perceive Heaven to be like in that moment.

I think that's why Jim and me have this connection; this unbreakable bond. I was reborn, all thanks to him."

A lump was forming in my throat. It sounded so perfect; if it wasn't for Jim, I would never have even got the chance to obsess over Aaron Holmes, let alone be here, out on tour with him.

"Did Jim turn the others too?"

"Nope, that was all my doing."

"So when, and where, did you find them?"

"Ask me what my favourite era was?" Aaron said, "Well at least up until now, anyway." He smiled over at me and took an almost gargantuan bite out of a hunk of bread and cheese.

"What was your favourite era?"

"Ah, funny you should ask actually," he mumbled round the food in his mouth, "The seventies were unreal; it was all about awesome music, free love and drugs – I did it all!"

"The 'free love' bit too?"

"Hell yeah," he answered, "and I'll let you in on a little secret too; I didn't *just* enjoy women."

I actually found that pretty easy to believe. Aaron has

this charm and charisma and along with devastatingly good looks, I could see why both women and men would want him.

"Oh okay, whatever floats your boat."

"Yup," he said, nodding proudly, "The whole world seemed to open up before me and I have to admit, I felt greedy."

"I wanted to try everything, Bea. I never thought of myself as gay, straight, bi or whatever. I was just me; always will be. Here's the thing though, I *never* fell in love back then, *never*. You're different though. This is so different," he paused for breath.

"The past is the past, Bea," he went on, "It's gone – it's done. I would really love for you to be my present and future."

He looked straight into my wide open eyes. It was a look that *screamed* of truth, honesty and sincerity.

All of a sudden, food didn't seem all that important. In fact, eating was the last thing on my mind. Had Aaron just said, in a round-about way, that he wanted me to be his girlfriend? Do vampires have such a thing? I was under the impression, whether it was fact *or* fantasy, that the only relationship they had with females was fleeting to say the very least – a *one in every port* kind of set up.

Aaron continued, recounting how he met Tim, Alex, Liam and Jack at a Cream gig and found they were almost bigger fans than he was. They ended up in a little pub in Soho; it got messy. They had an amazing time and although Aaron didn't want to ruin anything, he couldn't keep the guys in the dark about what he was.

It may have been that they were all high on drink and drugs or it may have been that they didn't believe a word Aaron had said, but the five stuck together, eventually holing up in a ramshackle apartment on the outskirts of Camden.

It was only once they began living together that he realised he had a ready-made band; Tim on drums, Alex on bass guitar, Liam on lead guitar and Jack on rhythm.

The apartment's top floor became their practice pad and studio and within months they had recorded and produced their very first demo. They passed it on to Jim, who had, in the meantime, single-handedly set up his own label, 'A Drop of Claret'.

"Aptly named, don't you think?" he said, "And that's how Shout the Call, or as we were originally known, The Night Walkers, came to be. We went through plenty of other names before that *and* our style of music *and* fashion changed on more than a few occasions, of course but our line-up was set in stone. It didn't matter what we were called or what we looked like, we were a band of brothers.

Without me, there would never have been a band and it was a band of best friends. We were so very close back in the day and one of the guys was keen on getting even closer."

If what he was telling me was 'on-the-record', it would have been the exclusive New Music; Non Stop would have killed for but it would also bring Vampires into the real world and I'm not sure whether it was ready for that just yet. I'm glad my morals have remained intact in this cut throat, sometimes seedy, industry.

"I understand if you prefer not to say but who was it, Aaron? Who wanted more?"

"Oh man, I don't know if I should say," Aaron paused. He looked deadly serious and it was obvious he wanted to tell me but did he trust me enough? "Bea, you have to swear you'll never tell a soul. The only other person that has any idea about this is Jim and he appreciates how important a secret it is."

"I do Aaron, I swear on my life!"

Chapter 11

"It was Jack who came to me first," Aaron said, "by then, all the band knew what I was and as far as I was aware, they were all pretty okay with it."

"But?" I asked.

"But Jack wasn't happy, Bea. He wanted a private chat and I knew what was coming."

"He wanted you to turn him, right?"

"Not straight away, no. We went out for beers and things got a bit messy. When we got home, everyone else was in bed but Jack and me, well – we weren't ready to call it a night."

Aaron looked down at his hands and I allowed my

eyes to follow his gaze. I looked back up to see his face turn suddenly serious.

"Are you okay?" I whispered.

"I'm fine, I suppose. It's just a sore subject, that's all. Anyway, after another few beers I got tired and told Jack I was going to go to bed but he had other plans. He pinned me hard against the wall and kissed me. It was full on.

"At first, I wanted to knock him into next week but I started to enjoy it; it's not like I hadn't been with men before. This was different though, totally different. Jack and I had always been the closest. There was always this kind of *bromance* between us. We were as thick as thieves and the rest of the band picked up on it as did the small horde of fans we had at the time."

Now he mentioned it, I had noticed that there was *something* between Jack and Aaron on stage but I just put it down to my over active imagination.

"Jack could sense I was getting a little too carried away. He knows full well what happens when I lose control," Aaron continued regretfully, "I pulled away the second my fangs made an appearance; it was all getting way too out of hand. Jack looked at me like I was out of my mind but begged me to bite him. I told him he was being a complete dick but he was insistent."

"Oh my God!" I exclaimed. Aaron shook his head.

"He said he wanted to be with me for eternity and I told him he hadn't got a clue what he was asking. Before I could say another word, he kissed me again, even harder than before. It was so easy to kiss back and this time I did nothing to try and calm myself down. When Jack showed me his neck, I did it – I bit him. I savoured every glorious drop that passed my lips. I practically drained him dry and then, just as Jim had urged me to, I made him drink my blood. He was my first willing victim and the rest of the band soon followed suit."

Aaron paid our bill, making it more than obvious he wanted to be out of there. It was good to actually be back outside; the fresh air is exactly what I needed. We walked back to the bus in almost contemplative silence. It seemed we both had a fair few things on our minds. I mean, I had followed them around the country. I went to as many gigs as I possibly could and only now, ten years on, did it suddenly dawn on me - Shout the Call have *never* aged. They've never looked any different and now I knew exactly why. By turning his four friends in the seventies. By making time stand still at a time they all enjoyed the most, he had cemented Shout the Call's future. He had preserved the band exactly as it was all those years ago.

"Jack knew how much I thought of him, Bea," Aaron said, picking up where he left off at the café, "but about a year or so later, we fell out – big time. He couldn't handle the fact that I wasn't just his; I never was. I did think a great deal of him and I think I did actually love him but being in a band brings attention and he just couldn't handle that. I don't think he's ever been able to."

"So, truthfully now - *do* you enjoy the attention or not?" I asked, having some idea of the jealousy Jack probably felt.

"No. No way," Aaron shot back, "don't get me wrong, the lads still partake in a little groupie activity here and there but it's not for me. I have to feed from the source occasionally, you saw that, but that's all it was and will ever be, especially now you're here. You've changed me, Bea."

He opened the bus door, pulling his coat off at the same time, which he tossed on to the sofa. He plonked himself down on to it and I copied. I turned to face him; we were centimetres away from each other.

"Aaron Holmes," I said, my voice thick with emotion, "I think I might just bloody love you."

"I know," he replied, "I think I might just bloody love you too."

Aaron pulled my hands away from his cheeks then gently held my face, pulling me to him. He planted a soft kiss on my forehead, then my mouth and immediately, softness went out of the window. Our passionate encounter ended abruptly as we heard someone cough sharply from the door.

Chapter 12

"Jack! You okay, mate?" Aaron asked, clearly embarrassed.

"I knew it," Jack spat at him and laughed, "I just knew there was something going on between you two. Why couldn't you just tell me, Aaron?"

"Should I have to tell you?" Aaron replied, "This has nothing to do with you, does it now?"

I winced, suddenly wanting to disappear, and let the two of them sort things out. After what we had just been talking about, Aaron really could have handled this better.

"Oh, it's nothing to do with me at all but I'm just not a huge fan of walking in on my man and his new piece of meat."

"Jack, what the fuck is wrong with you, dude?" Aaron shouted as he got up and walked towards him, "I don't know where you got this notion from – we were never a *couple*!"

"Oh really," Jack said as he got right up into Aaron's face, "You weren't saying that all those times we were *together*!"

"Oh piss off will you, it's not like we were married! I've always liked you, Jack, really liked you but that's it; it's as simple as that."

I was feeling more uncomfortable by the second. I felt like an intruder.

"Guys, I'm going to leave," I butted in quickly, "you two need to sort this out and I don't think you can do that while I'm here." I stood up to go but Aaron pulled me back.

"You will not, Bea," he said as he pulled me to his chest, "you've as much right to be here as either of us. I have nothing to hide."

"I know you don't," I said gently, "but I really think it's for the best. We have plenty of time to be together. You need to talk."

"Actually, Bea, forget it," Jack spat at me, "you're welcome to the piece of shit – he's all yours. Just a word to the wise though; be prepared to have your heart broken!" And with that, he was gone.

Chapter 13

"Let it go, Bea," Aaron said as I made to follow after Jack, "let him get on with it."

"I know what you're saying, Aaron but I do feel a little to blame in all of this. I've come into the fold and I can kind of understand him."

"He's just jealous, that's all. He knows how much I'm into you."

"Obviously," I said, feeling slightly smug, "that's as plain as the nose on your face. Don't you feel even a hint of guilt?"

"What the hell for?" Aaron shouted, making it clear that I had hit a nerve, "I haven't got anything to prove or justify. I was never exclusively his; never have been, never will."

Aaron was completely right, of course but I still felt bad for Jack.

"I know that, Aaron but please don't let it lie like this," I replied, "You're a tight band, great friends *and* you have a gig tonight; at least try and clear some air for that."

"And you think Jack's going to listen to a single word I say?"

"I don't know whether you've noticed, honey," I answered, "but he hangs on your every word. I also know you think a lot of him as he does of you too. Sort it out, Aaron or you'll regret it forever."

Aaron's silence was deafening. He was waging a war within himself; he was totally right yet wrong all the same. He cursed under his breath, sighed and stormed out after his best friend.

******

There were three other photographers with me; a fact that excited me. There's always a friendly competition and banter when there's a few of you rushing around in a narrow space.

Anticipation was building quickly amongst the crowd but it felt different somehow. The crowd was, if it was possible, even more eager than usual. The chants of 'Shout the Call' began low and deep but quickly escalated to screams as the house lights went out and the band barrelled on stage. After shooting, we all filed out of the pit. I introduced myself to the other three and we swapped business cards without even thinking and parted ways.

The bar was an oasis at the back of the room full of hot, sweaty and rather smelly gig goers. I ordered a beer and downed it in four mouthfuls. I covered my mouth and hoped the emerging, post gulp burp would get lost in the sound of Shout the Call's encore.

I ordered another drink but took my time with it - enough time to see the encore out to the end. I cheered and clapped along with everyone else in the room as the five guys on stage waved and bowed and threw drumsticks, plectrums and bottles of water out to whoever could catch them.

I was filled with a sense of pride as I made my way backstage and I wasn't watching at all where I was going as I headed down the harsh, neon lit corridor to our room so the startled yelp I let out was no surprise as I slammed, almost head on, into Jack.

"I'm so sorry," I stuttered.

"Just watch where you're fucking going, huh?" Jack

spat angrily.

I looked at him in shock; there really was no need for that, especially after I had apologised.

"Look, I know you're upset about earlier," I said, quickly stopping myself from saying too much more. I didn't want to let on that I knew what had happened between the two of them.

"Why would I be upset?" he asked, maybe sensing that I knew more than I probably should.

"Oh, no reason," I answered, hoping I could come back with a believable retort, "It's just not something you want to walk in on, is it really?"

"Can't say I'm bothered to be honest, Beatrice," Jack replied and by using my full name, I knew he meant business.

"Cool," I replied simply, beginning to feel fear well up in my chest.

"Well, actually – no, it's not!" Jack shouted through gritted teeth and clenched jaw, "You think Aaron likes you? You really think he wants you?"

"Although it has absolutely nothing at all to do with you; yes – I think he does," I answered angrily.

Jack laughed; it was dramatic and false.

"For God's sake, Bea, Aaron is a vampire – we all are."

"And?"

"Surely you've seen all the shitty movies and read all those godforsaken books?" Jack asked, irritated.

"I've watched a few, yes."

"We drink blood," he replied. I rolled my eyes, how boring. To think I had come to a point when all this seemed *boring* was pretty unreal. Jack went on, "We drain idiot human beings, much like you, of it."

Even though I didn't want to get any angrier, I couldn't help it and Jack knew full well he was causing chinks to appear in my armour.

"Cool. Thanks for the lovely chat, Jack. I really have enjoyed it but while you go off and drain some *idiot human beings* like me, I think I'll go and help myself to hospitality. Knock 'em dead." I turned to walk away but not before noticing his irritated expression. It was clear he didn't like my attempt at sarcasm.

His face suddenly turned evil as he threw me up against the wall. He pinned me to the spot, leaving me absolutely no room to maneuver out of his grasp.

"He only wants you for one thing, you know that

right? So what's say I beat him to it?" He whispered into my ear before he pulled my head to one side, exposing my neck. I felt his breath tickle my skin and then his lips brush over it.

I shut my eyes tight and just as I braced myself for the inevitable; I heard a *thwack* and Jack dropped to the floor. I opened my eyes to see Aaron standing in front of me, behind Jack's crumpled heap of a body; he brandished a baseball bat in his right hand.

"You okay?" he asked, shaking with anger and adrenaline.

"I am now."

Chapter 14

"Oh my God," I said, looking at Jack, who was flat out on the floor, "is he going to be okay?"

"You're telling me you care about that shit bag?" Aaron replied, confused and somewhat shocked.

"Well, kind of - a little bit."

"For Christ's sake, he's just tried to drain you!"

"I know that, Aaron. I'm not stupid," I said, puzzled by my sudden defensiveness of Jack, "You guys have been through too much together. I don't want to be the one who ruins that.

"You're out of your mind, you know that?!" Aaron spat at me, shaking his head and laughing.

My throat became thick and I struggled to keep tears back.

"Please, Aaron," I said, my voice shaking, "don't talk to me like a child. I'm more than aware of the situation and the surroundings I'm in. I'm far from out of my mind."

Aaron's demeanour shifted almost immediately. He knew I was no fool and that my head was screwed on the right way. He pulled me to his chest and held me as though he would never let me go. He let out a deep, heavy sigh.

"Oh, Bea, I'm sorry, honey. I'm just wound up. Just put yourself in my shoes though; you would have done the same, right?"

"Maybe not exactly," I replied, "I don't think I would have had the balls to do what you just did but yes, it would definitely have got my back up."

"Would it make you feel any better if we wait until he comes round?" Aaron asked reluctantly before placing a tender kiss on my forehead.

"Oh, so he will come round then?" I asked, smiling cheekily, "because that blow would have rendered any mere mortal extinct."

We both laughed and stepped over to the opposite

wall. We rested our backs to it and sank down to sitting positions.

"You realise we might be here a while, right?" Aaron asked, leaning into me.

"Oh well, never mind," I replied, "I spy with my little eye..."

******

Jack winced and groaned as he unfurled himself; his bones seemed to crunch, almost as if they were resetting themselves.

"So nice of you to join us," Aaron said as he stood up. He stepped over to Jack and kicked his feet sharply, "enjoyed your nap?"

"What?" Jack replied, sounding drunk, "What happened?"

"How very convenient," Aaron replied, turning to look at me out of the corner of his eye. Jack still looked utterly bemused.

"What the hell are you going on about?"

"Oh, so I assume you don't remember me catching you trying to drain Bea?"

I half expected Jack to look disgusted, maybe even shocked but no.

"And?" Jack replied, rubbing his jaw, "Because we all know that's the only reason she's really here, right?"

"Fuck you, Jack," Aaron shouted, right up in his face.

"Ooh, someone's getting riled. Hit a nerve, have I?"

"Bea, get out of here," Aaron urged but I was in no way ready to leave.

"Um, I don't think so," I shot in, "I think I have more than a right to be here, don't you?"

"Don't argue with me, not now. Please, just get out of here."

I couldn't quite believe what I was doing but I stood rigid; nailed to the spot. My stubbornness was kicking in.

"Actually," Jack said, interrupting our little lover's tiff, "I personally think its best that Beatrice hangs around. It's about time she heard some home truths."

"What truths would those be then Jack?"

"You know damn well what, Aaron!"

"Oh, I think I know what this is all about, Bea," Aaron said, turning to me.

"Jack, I know about you and Aaron," I said, stopping my boyfriend from going any further. Jack's face dropped and any amount of smugness he may have been feeling quickly disappeared.

"What have you done? What have you told her?" he shouted at Aaron, grabbing hold of his shirt and yanking him towards him.

"The truth" he replied with a smirk, "and nothing but the truth, so help me God."

"You bastard, Aaron!" Jack spat.

"What's the matter mate; I thought you wanted Bea to know everything?"

Jack could not deny it and therefore had no argument. He had no words. Aaron seized his opportunity to gloat.

"Yes, she knows everything and I mean *everything*," Aaron confirmed, "that's what you do when you love someone, Jack; you talk to them."

This wasn't awkward at all.

"You don't love her, Aaron; she's only here because you want to feed on her. It's that simple."

"Change the bloody record, Jack. This shit's boring the hell out of me now," Aaron said, and the look on Jack's face suggested he knew he was losing the battle.

"Now," Aaron continued, "even though you've pissed me off, and believe me, my friend, that is a pretty epic understatement, I'm willing to put this shit to bed. No matter what, we are Shout the Call and whether you like it or not, we're bound by contract to tour the hell out of this record. Oh, and also, you're my best friend in this world. So, let's just get back to business, shall we?"

I immediately felt incredibly proud; it takes a big person to offer out the proverbial olive branch, especially when they're not even the slightest bit in the wrong. Aaron extended his hand to Jack. Jack grabbed it and shook it strongly before he was pulled into a tight hug.

Jack stared straight at me with a sinister smirk plastered across his face.

******

"What the hell's going on?" Jim shouted as he slammed the door open into the corridor. His eyes darted between Aaron and Jack.

"Nothing, mate, just something that we needed to sort out, isn't that right, Jack?"

Jack smiled and nodded and it gave me goosebumps - not the good type.

"And is it sorted now?" Jim asked them both.

"Yes, I promise. Scouts honour," Aaron replied making the appropriate salute, "best friends forever again now." He put his arm around Jack's shoulder - a visual display, just to hammer the point home.

"Right, okay," Jim said, walking up to me and putting his arm around my shoulders, "Bea, are you okay, love?"

"I'm fine, Jim, thank you."

"Good," he said, looking at me as if he knew I wasn't telling the whole truth, "I'm off to the nearest bar and I'm going to sink a few. A change of scenery is exactly what I need and I haven't got to be up too early tomorrow morning, so yeah. See you all later."

"Yeah, I'm off too," Jack added, although where he planned on disappearing off to was not forthcoming.

I stood there silent and somewhat shell-shocked. The night had been a roller coaster. The highs were so very high and the one low part was very, very low.

"I love you, Bea," Aaron said, his voice guiding me

off the ride and to safety.

"Love you too," I replied.

Chapter 15

"Look, I'm not ready to call it a night yet, honey, are you?" Aaron asked as we slowly strolled down the pavement outside the venue, towards the bus, "You fancy going on to a club?"

"Would you mind if I said no?"

Aaron looked at me, concerned and confused. "What's the matter? You still got all that business on your mind?" he said, obviously referring to the kerfuffle earlier.

"I suppose so. A little bit," I half agreed, "to be honest though, it's more the fact that I'm tired and don't think I'd be the best of company. I just want to get back to my bunk, chill out and maybe have a beer or two there."

"Actually, that sounds like a great idea. To be fair, it wouldn't do me any harm to call it a night either," he said, "bloody hell, listen to me being all responsible and shit. Do you and your bunk want some company?"

"I wouldn't say no."

"Cool," he said as we rounded the corner and saw the bus come into view, "you carry on in though and I'll go and get a take away or something. Any preference?"

"Surprise me," I said as I pecked him on the cheek, leaving him as I jogged to the bus.

******

With a bottle of beer in hand, I headed to my bunk and plonked myself down. I really could have done with getting my photos edited and out the way but I just didn't have it in me.

I grabbed a pen from out of my safe box and took out my writing pad. It was time to try and finish the book I had been working on before I got this job. I needed to get it published; I needed to put it to bed. I pulled my iPod out from my travel bag along with my headphones. I set my music to shuffle and quickly got into writing mode; the words began flowing from my pen on to the crisp, white, lined paper. I became so lost in the writing and my music that I never heard the bus door open and never sensed the presence in the room until it stood there, right in front of me.

******

"Jesus, Jack, you scared the crap out of me!" I exclaimed, catching my breath.

"Did I? I'm so sorry," he said falsely.

I watched him closely, unbelieving as he pushed my legs off the side of my bunk so he could sit down. He sat way too close for comfort; more than invading my personal space.

"Whatcha doing?" he asked, snatching my writing pad from my hands. "Ooh, what's all this about then?"

Jack's eyes darted back and forth. Whether he was actually reading or faking it, I really couldn't tell but I had this unnerving feeling that something bad was brewing.

"Oh, okay so you think you're a writer or something?" Jack asked, laughing as he flicked through page after page.

"Well, it's just a bit of a hobby really," I answered gingerly, "but yes, I consider myself a writer. I've already had one book published and I'm pretty proud of it actually."

"Proud? Oh right," Jack laughed, "I don't know why that is; I've only glanced over a page of this and I already know it's going to be a load of crap!"

"Well, it's just a rough draft," I replied, angry at myself for even justifying my work to him.

"Babe, regardless of that," Jack said seriously, "you know that saying, don't you? You can't polish a turd!"

I saw red instantly and felt pure anger rise up inside me. I wanted to retaliate with a witty, cutting remark but I couldn't get past the feeling that I could happily strangle him.

"What is your problem?" I asked, already knowing the answer, of course, "I know you're pissed at me and Aaron and I know you're angry, maybe even a little jealous."

"Jealous? Ha! You think I give a shit about you, you stupid bitch?" Jack said as he grabbed my throat and pushed me backwards on my bed. He moved in to a kneeling position, pressing down harder on my throat as he straddled my hips. I felt my breath become short in a matter of seconds.

"Jack," I said between gulps of precious air, "what are you doing? If Aaron finds out….."

Jack bellowed a deep, low laugh.

"Your boyfriend is off doing his thing, honey. You're deluded if you think he gives a damn about you! If I were you, I'd bear that in mind the next time he declares his, excuse the pun, undying love for you. I don't know how many times I will have to drum that into that thick skull of yours; *he doesn't love you*! He has never loved anyone and he's not about to start. It's not in his nature; it's not in a vampire's nature."

"Look, Jack," I heaved as he switched between applying more pressure and loosening his grip, "you can say what you want; you can think what you want but I choose not to believe you." I stopped to suck in another breath, "If you don't like that, then do your worst!"

For the second time, Jack's mouth was on me; on my ear first, breathing heavily into it. He pushed my head to the right, squashing my mouth into my pillow. If I couldn't breathe properly before, I really couldn't now. I felt the sharp sting of Jack's teeth at my neck as I closed my eyes, bracing myself. Somewhere in the background, I heard the bus door slam open. Before I could see who was there, my whole world turned black.

Chapter 16

"Bea, honey, can you hear me?" I heard someone say although I couldn't be exactly sure if what I heard was real or a dream. I must have been asleep; all I could see was darkness. I tried to open my eyes but they weren't complying.

"Bea. Can you hear me?" the voice spoke again and this time, I felt a flicker of recognition. It was Aaron; yes, it was definitely him.

I forced once more and my eyes opened and then I felt intense relief and happiness as I saw his face above me, looking down like a guardian angel. I opened my mouth to speak, to tell Aaron exactly how much I loved him but nothing; no sound wanted to come out. Tears began to fill my eyes and cloud my vision.

"Hey, shush," Aaron said, bending down and planting a kiss on my clammy forehead, "don't try to speak, honey. It's okay."

I looked around the room and saw Jim slouched in a rather uncomfortable looking chair. He was snoring quietly. I suddenly realised I was in hospital. The room was devoid of any character, looking too clinical to be calming. The only colour in the bright white room was the bouquet of roses on the windowsill. I looked at Aaron and nodded towards the blood red flowers, silently asking if they were for me. Aaron understood and nodded.

"Do you like them?" he asked.

I nodded back, wishing my voice would make a swift return. My mouth and throat felt as dry as the Sahara, something which Aaron picked up on instantly as he poured a cup of water, dropping a straw into it.

"Here," he said as he gently guided the straw to my dry, chapped lips, "you must be thirsty."

I had always underestimated water really. I mean, it's just so plain and well, nothing, but the moment that first flood of water filled my mouth, it truly was the best thing I had ever tasted. I guzzled and slugged at it greedily. Aaron slowly drew the straw back out of my mouth.

"What are you doing?" I choked, realising I was finally talking even though I sounded like I had been smoking a hundred cigarettes a day.

"I'm sorry, sweetheart," Aaron answered, smiling awkwardly, "try not to overload your system straight away. Just small sips okay?"

"Okay," I replied, swallowing to soothe my throat, "I'm sorry."

Aaron looked at me in complete disbelief. Was he about to start crying?

"No. No you don't!" he said, his voice quivering; confirming my suspicion. "You have nothing to be sorry about. If anything, it should be me saying sorry. In fact, I really should be begging for your forgiveness."

Jim let out a bellowing snort and I half expected him to wake himself up but he simply carried on with his deep, uncomfortable looking sleep.

"What are *you* saying sorry for?" I asked back, wearing exactly the same look of disbelief that Aaron had done before me.

"If it wasn't for me, you wouldn't be on the road with us; you wouldn't know what we are and therefore you wouldn't be lying here, in a hospital bed."

He dropped his head on to my chest and I felt the wetness of his tears on my skin. I submerged my face into his mass of soft, unruly curls. Even though I could have happily stayed that way forever, I moved his hair out of the way and, placing both hands on his cheeks, I lifted his face. His brown-green eyes bored into mine, searching for forgiveness; forgiveness that really wasn't required.

"Aaron, please don't," I said, stroking his cheeks with my thumbs, "I *could* have said no to this gig. It wasn't exclusive to me. My boss gave me first refusal because he knows how much I love you guys; he knows how obsessed I am with the lead singer. There is no way on God's earth that I would ever have passed this up."

"Yeah but I should have been straight with New Music; Non Stop from the get go."

"Right, and that would have really won you the coverage, wouldn't it?" I said, "Can you imagine? 'Hi, I'm Aaron Holmes, lead singer of Shout the Call. We'd like full coverage of our European headline tour. Oh, I forgot to mention; we're a bunch of blood-sucking vampires!"

Aaron's smile grew from a tiny little smirk to a full on, wide grin. We both burst into laughter; finding joy in a pretty ridiculous situation.

"I love you, Bea, a lot." he said as he leant in towards me, placing a long, deep, lingering kiss on my mouth.

"I love you too" I replied sincerely, kissing him like it was the last kiss I would ever have.

Chapter 17

"Do you remember what happened?" Aaron asked as he tucked me into my bunk.

"I wish I didn't," I replied truthfully as images of Jack and what he did to me flashed through my mind.

"Look, I know the last thing you will want to do tomorrow is work," Aaron continued, "and I have a feeling the last place you'll want to be is on the bus. If you can just bear with it for tonight, whilst we travel, I'll sort a nice hotel or apartment in Hamburg tomorrow when we get there."

"Hamburg?" I asked sleepily, "Another place I've never been."

"I'm still amazed you actually want to be here," he said, a mixture of shock and sadness tainting his tone.

"Of course! As long as I'm with you, I'm happy," I replied. One little vampire bite wouldn't tear this girl away. "Have you heard from Jack?"

"I have, whilst the doctor was discharging you earlier," he said.

"And?"

"And I told him he is no longer a member of Shout the Call," Aaron answered firmly. "What he did was evil; he could have killed you."

"Actually, that's what I've been meaning to ask," I said, casting my mind to all the films I had seen, the general rule of thumb being that unless the vampire that bit you gave you their own blood, you had no chance. "How am I not dead Aaron? Why am I still here? Am I immortal now?"

Aaron looked down at his hands. His thumbs were twiddling nervously.

"I am, aren't I?" I went on, "answer me, please."

"No," Aaron replied shortly, "You were given a blood transfusion; standard practice if you lose a lot of the red stuff."

I looked at him questionably.

"Are you telling me the truth?" I asked, noting how on edge he seemed.

"Yes," he replied, looking straight at me; his face all serious.

"About Jack," I said and paused, feeling awkward, "you can't get rid of him; he's a founding member of the band."

"Christ, Bea - not this again!" Aaron snapped, "The guy seriously crossed the line this time round. He doesn't deserve any more chances and certainly any more bloody sympathy, from you especially."

I took his hands in mine.

"I know that, honey, and what he did was completely, utterly wrong but I'm pretty sure he knows that and what he could lose. He wouldn't dare to cross me again. Just speak to him, let him know exactly how you feel and give him his final warning. I know I sound like a broken record, but you've been through too much to just give up."

"You honestly think that's wise?" he asked, half shaking his head in disbelief.

"Maybe, maybe not; all I know is that you're such an amazing band and I can't really imagine it without Jack, no matter what he's done."

"Are you absolutely sure about this?" Aaron asked, looking utterly torn, "it means he'll be back on the bus let alone sharing the stage with us."

"I'm aware of that," I yawned and hoped Aaron didn't think I was bored with him.

"You're tired," Aaron stated, quite obviously.

"Very. Now get on the phone; speak to Jack. Like I said before, you'll regret it if you don't. But," I added as an afterthought, "don't make it easy for him. Make him grovel – give him hell!"

He nodded reluctantly and kissed my forehead and within seconds, his face faded from view as my eyes gave up the fight to stay open and I fell to sleep.

Chapter 18

I woke to the muffled sound of Aaron and Jim talking outside the bus and gentle tapping on my left hand. As I came to, I saw Jack sitting on the side of my bunk. I recoiled as he touched my arm, hoping that Aaron would somehow telepathically sense I was unhappy with my visitor; hoping that he would kick the door down and save me like some valiant knight in shining armour.

"Hi, Jack," I said firmly.

"Hi. So, I just wanted to apologise for well, you know," Jack stammered awkwardly.

"No, I don't know," I replied, "Please enlighten me." Although I really didn't want to get into any kind of in depth conversation with him, I was angry and he was the last person I wanted to see.

"What I did was despicable; completely and utterly wrong." Jack went on.

"Yes it was."

"And I am not asking for your forgiveness…"

"Good!" I interrupted, feeling more than a little dubious about his somewhat sudden change of heart.

"I just wanted you to know that I really am so sorry, Bea; I don't know what came over me."

"You were jealous, Jack; I think that's what did it." I said sarcastically. Jack looked down at his hands, knowing full well I was right.

"That'd be it, yes. You're a great girl and Aaron obviously thinks the world of you and I am so sorry."

"Apology accepted," I said, putting my hands over his, "but you know me and Aaron are very much together and as much as I will try to keep myself in check when it comes to public displays of affection, it will be impossible to completely avoid. Do you understand?"

"I do," he replied, nodding, "I understand very well but I have to tell you this too; I loved Aaron with every fibre of my being. I would have done absolutely anything and everything for him, so believe me when I say I know how much you love him."

"That's why I need you to put your jealousy to the back of your mind," I said sympathetically, "this is how it is now."

"I know that, Bea. You know, I'm amazed Aaron actually phoned me and even more amazed that he's let me back in the band. He told me it was you who changed his mind and I told him he had a very special girl in you. Thank you; I mean that, truly."

"Good," I said firmly, "I didn't do it for you though, let me make that clear. I just want this band to stay together. It's a simple as that."

Jack smiled awkwardly and nodded.

"Just one last thing," I added, stretching my tired, aching muscles, "don't even dare to try anything like that again, okay?"

Jack gave a Scout's salute and headed for the door.

******

"Hey, honey," Aaron greeted as I alighted the

empty tour bus for some much needed fresh air.

"Hey," I replied. He pulled me into his all encompassing embrace and kissed my nose.

"So, Jack spoke to you huh?" Aaron asked as he pulled away.

"He did."

"Did everything go okay?"

"It was fine." I answered, smiling at him reassuringly.

"So, you slept all the way to Hamburg, Bea," Aaron said, thankfully changing the subject, "you must have been *super* tired."

I looked around me, bewildered to find we had most definitely relocated. I obviously must have needed the rest.

"Now look," Aaron went on, "me and Jim, well, we've come to a mutual decision – you're definitely not working tonight."

"But," I tried, yet failed, to interrupt.

"No you don't," he went on, shaking his right index finger at me. "You, my dear, are *not* coming to work tonight. You've been through enough over these last few days. As promised, I have booked a lovely hotel. This evening, our home will be the Hotel Am Dammtor. Our room will be ready at three and we'll be staying there tonight and tomorrow night too because we're doing a signing session and acoustic set at Thomas Read Irish Pub in Reeperbahn tomorrow afternoon."

"A signing session? Since when?" I asked, "I didn't have that down on the itinerary Jim gave me."

"That's because it wasn't on there, Bea. We only found out about it last night. We had an email from the guy who runs Logo; the place we're playing tonight. He had a load of fans wanting 'meet and greet' tickets but he told them it wasn't something they do. He put forward the idea to Jim, which he jumped at. Let's just say, we'll make pretty much the same amount of money tomorrow, for a few hours work than we do in one gig and all we have to do is chat to fans. It's going to be an 'up close and personal' thing and about two hundred fans have paid for the privilege."

"See, I told you I'm not the only woman in history that wants your body. You'll be beating them off with a stick!"

Aaron looked at me awkwardly; yet again, it seemed I had hit a nerve in regards to his 'fans'.

"I'm just kidding." I continued.

"Oh right," he replied, forcing a laugh, "I knew that."

"So, I'm being banished to a hotel room for the night then?"

"Not just any room, Bea. It's a five star establishment, I'll have you know," he answered, unable to pull back the giggle about to escape his mouth.

"Five star eh? Well, I have nothing to complain about then, have I."

"Exactly!" Aaron replied, looking more than a little pleased with himself.

"Well thank you, honey, I really appreciate it but it kind of sucks too," I said, immediately noticing the look of disappointment on his face, "I really wanted to see you tonight at Logo; it has quite the reputation. It's supposed to be renowned for putting on some amazing rock acts."

Aaron looked dumbfounded; how did I know. Of course, it's all part and parcel of doing what I do. I have to do my research.

"Yeah, it is," Aaron said, "but don't you think you need to just relax tonight? You have the comfort of a king size bed, which of course, I'll be joining you in after the gig."

I looked at Aaron with my best 'puppy-dog' eyes and pouted like my life depended on it.

"Don't," Aaron said.

"What?"

"Don't do that," he replied.

"Whatever could you mean?" I asked again, out-pouting my previous attempt.

"That thing," he replied, pointing at my face and circling his finger in front of me.

"What, this?" I asked, demonstrating 'the face' again.

"Okay, okay; will you come to Logo tonight?"

"Hallelujah!" I replied, raising my hands to the sky, "You got it in one." I rolled my eyes and giggled.

"Well you're not working if you do," he ordered, "No offence but I don't want you there at all and I only say that because I seriously think you need to rest but *nothing* I say is going to stop you, is it?"

"Nope!"

"So, you're just going to come and watch us play?" Aaron asked, looking more confused by the second. Did he think I only ever went to gigs if I got a photo pass?

"Yup," I answered, "in fact, I can't think of anything better right now."

Aaron tipped his head back and laughed before quickly turning serious.

"Every song tonight, Bea; I'll sing every one for you and when I sprint off that stage, straight to you I will give you a big, hot, sweaty squeeze. How very Mills and Boon," he said, breaking down into giggles as he acted out exactly what he was going to do to me before whispering breathlessly into my ear, "and then, I will drag you backstage, into the bathroom, where I will have a quick shower – you might even want to join me. Then we'll go back to the hotel and show that king size bed a thing or two - only if you feel okay. How does that sound?"

My skin prickled with goose bumps as he trailed light kisses down my neck and onto my clavicle.

"Perfect."

Chapter 19

When Aaron said the hotel was five star, he really wasn't wrong. It was amazing and resplendent and we were staying in it for the next two nights.

Matching 'his and hers' bathrobes were laid out on the bed and over on the large, ornate dressing table that took up most of the bay window, there was a Welcome tray full with chocolates, strawberries and a bottle of champagne; it all felt a little too good for little old me.

There were four hours to kill before I headed out to Logo and at first, I really wasn't quite sure what to do with myself but then I decided to pop open the fizz and break into the goodies.

I guzzled down a glass of champagne and

immediately started to feel myself lagging. I couldn't still be tired after sleeping over twelve hours and entering a whole different country, could I?

******

Damn it; I must have been tired, I thought to myself as I looked at my watch. It was five thirty and I had exactly an hour and a half to haul my backside out of bed, get showered, changed and of course, made up. My phone buzzed to life as it received a text message.

"Hope you're ready for tonight sugar xxx."

"Almost," I typed in, ***"Can't wait to see you. Now let me get ready and please do not disturb again; it takes time to look this beautiful!"***

Aaron's reply came quickly.

"OK honey. Bye for now xxx."

I got a room call from reception explaining a taxi was outside, waiting for me. Now, that I was not expecting. Calling a cab hadn't even crossed my mind whilst I was busy trying to make myself look presentable. I rushed out, making sure the door was locked before putting the key card deep down into a secret zip pocket in my bag. I climbed into the back of the car seconds before the driver put his foot down and we made our way to Logo.

Jim was standing outside the main entrance as we pulled up; he put his cigarette out as soon as he saw me. I ran straight up to him and gave him a huge hug.

"What are you doing here, Bea?" he asked, "Didn't Aaron tell you you had the night off?"

"He did but I'm a very persuasive gal," I said lightheartedly, "And anyway, going to a gig isn't *working* now, is it?"

"Bloody hell, Bea," he sighed, seemingly annoyed that I was purposefully ignoring their wishes, "just be careful then will you?"

"I promise! Don't worry, Aaron gave me the talk," I said, smiling, "you know, Jim; I haven't always done this job. I've always enjoyed going to gigs, even before New Music. I just want to see my favourite band as a *fan* again and a fan is surely what I am."

"You sound like something out of a Dr Seuss book."

"I do, don't I?" I said, laughing at Jim's reference, "but it's going to be so cool to be in the thick of it tonight. I can soak it all in properly."

"Fair enough," Jim said, "I guess I can understand

that; you going somewhere after the gig?"

"Just back to the hotel he's booked us in to. What do you have planned?"

"Oh, just the usual really - back to the bus for a beer or two."

I nodded, smiled and gave him a quick peck on the cheek.

"Anyway, I guess I'll catch you later," I said, "I best go and take my place with the great unwashed."

Jim flashed me a wide smile and I headed through the doors.

******

The place was literally heaving with bodies, mainly women with groups of men propping up the bar which is exactly where I was headed. I was shocked at the distinct lack of bar staff; just two young looking girls, struggling to keep up with demand and heckles of half drunk, irritated, impatient punters. I felt the girls' pain; I knew only too well what they were going through. Just as I was about to offer them help, being the Good Samaritan that I am, I felt familiar, strong arms wrap around my waist. I shuddered as I felt Aaron's breath in my ear.

"Hey, baby," he whispered, causing my skin to prickle. He spun me round so that our noses were almost touching. He had his hood up, almost completely obscuring his face, Luckily, the gaggle of girls that had been, just minutes ago, declaring their undying love for Shout the Call's lead singer, didn't bat an eyelid - they just wanted to get their drinks in before the support came on.

He drew me away from the bar, right to the back of the room, out into the foyer and into the *Ladies* toilets. He didn't seem at all bothered that someone might see us but thankfully, the clinical, bright white room was empty. He gently pushed me into a cubicle.

"Hey, you," I smiled and kissed him deeply. Everything about the atmosphere between us, his smell and of course, the way he looked just intoxicated my every sense. I couldn't help it. "What time you going on?"

"Oh, we'll be hitting the stage about nine," he answered, smothering my neck with soft, butterfly kisses.

"Don't you think you ought to put me down then and go get ready?" I asked, not particularly wanting the affection and adoration to end, but happy it had to at the same time.

"Don't sweat it, honey. We know this shit like the back of our hands; we've got our timings down to a fine art."

"Cool. Anyway, if you don't mind, I just want to sink a few beers and enjoy the support on my own."

"Okay, okay," Aaron huffed, "if that's how you feel." We both laughed at how we were trying, yet failing miserably, to be aloof.

"Who is it, by the way; the support?" I asked.

"I haven't got a bloody clue tonight, honey; some local band. The venue's management sorted that out, and anyway, you don't need to watch them on your own – we don't go on for another hour yet. What if I want to watch them with you? I'll only grace you with my presence for half an hour, if that."

"And risk being mobbed by a bunch of over-excited, crazy fans?"

"Didn't you know I'm a master of disguise? I mean, look at this hood and how I hang my head low. Okay, not as convincing as I thought. I guess you're right." Aaron said, smiling in his defeat.

I nodded as he slipped his arm protectively around my shoulders and kissed my forehead.

******

Shout the Call hit the stage to howling, ear-splitting screams once again and I remembered exactly how it felt to be part of the 'experience'. Within moments of the first power chord being struck, I felt giddy; not through alcohol but pure adrenaline and elation. For some reason, I felt like I was seeing everything in high definition; my eyes felt wide open, as if I couldn't take enough in. My ears were somehow picking up so much more than the music blaring out over the PA. It sounded like people were whispering their conversations straight into them but as I turned around, trying to see who may have been getting a little too close for comfort, I only saw a room full of completely zoned out gig goers, enjoying the gig, just like me. I wondered if they were feeling what I was.

Then I felt a deep, intense sense of pure, physical hunger. I was ravenous, almost nauseous with it. I was super aware of every single body in the room; I could hear blood coursing through veins. I was totally unsure of what to do with myself; how to stand, where to put my hands. I couldn't concentrate on my boyfriend and the band; the only thing on my mind was how incredibly close every sweaty body in the room was to me. I gulped back the remnants of my beer and ran, like my life depended on it, out of the room.

My body slammed against the brisk, cold air as I tumbled out of the club. I doubled over, gasping – taking in as much oxygen as my lungs could handle. Was this a panic attack? It certainly showed all the hallmarks of one and that's when a deep realisation hit me; had Aaron lied to me when he told me I'd had a blood transfusion? I wasn't. I couldn't be, could I…

Chapter 20

As I let the rain pitter-patter on my upturned face, hoping it would calm me down, I heard a voice coming from behind me.

"Beatrice," Jim said, patting my back gently, "what's the matter, chick?"

I wanted to shout and ball at him; I thought I could trust him, hell, I thought I could trust him more than Aaron. How could he betray me like this? I knew though that no amount of screaming and shouting would help anything.

"Oh, hi, Jim," I answered through gritted teeth, "I'm fine, honestly. I think it all got a bit too much for me in there. I just needed a breather."

"Okay, chick, I get ya," he replied, "I can appreciate it. I mean, I bet you rarely have chance to get in the thick of it because of your job."

I clenched my jaw, angry at his assumption. Was he being intentionally patronising or was I just in a very bad mood?

"Oh, I'm not sure about that, Jim and anyway, I've been to more than my fair share of gigs as a punter so I think I still remember how it feels."

Jim smiled and gave my shoulders a squeeze. I let out a fake, strained laugh; that's all I could allow to come from my mouth.

"Seriously though, Bea," Jim went on, "you sure you're okay?"

"I'm fine, really."

"Good girl. Now are you coming back in?"

"You know what? No, I think I'm just going to head back to our hotel."

"It's really nice you're getting some alone time together, especially after what happened with Jack the other night. I honestly haven't seen Aaron this happy in a very long time. I do believe he's smitten."

"He is, is he?" I asked, unable to stop the hint of a

smile spreading across my face. Jim had redeemed himself almost instantly, "Well I do believe I am too. Hey, can you tell Aaron I'm sorry for not sticking around and I'll see him later?"

"Course I will, chick and I'm sure he'll race back after the gig once he knows you're waiting there for him."

Jim shot me a knowing wink before opening the double doors and disappearing back into the club.

******

Half of me wanted to kick off big time at Aaron; some blood transfusion, eh? How could I have been so naive? The other half of me wanted to wrap myself around him; couldn't wait to tell him I felt exactly the same as he did, if he didn't already know.

I removed my makeup and brushed my teeth. I decided upon the non-suggestive pair of plaid pj's that I packed; at least then, Aaron would take me seriously at a time I really needed to be. I just needed to keep my head in the game; I needed to keep my cool. My resolve started to slip, however, and I felt my eyelids begin to droop. It was just too much effort to keep them open.

The sound of bumping and tumbling woke me. I shot off the bed and grabbed Aaron just before he fell to the floor. It was clear he was drunk.

"Beatrice," he sang in a cheesy, opera style, "my Beatrice; where have you been my gorgeous, amazing beauty Queen."

It took every fibre of my being to stifle the giggle threatening to escape my mouth; but I wouldn't let myself crack.

"I've been here; waiting for you."

He sashayed up to me, pulling me to his chest and kissing my nose.

"And what a wonderful thing that is; I've never had anyone to come home to."

He may have been drunk but he was quickly softening my stern resolve.

"Jim said you left early," he hiccuped, "how come, honey?"

I couldn't push him away, or maybe I just didn't want to, as he smothered me in soft kisses. I moaned with pleasure as they travelled down my neck. How could I be angry with him when he was doing that?

"I just needed to get out of there," I replied

breathlessly, "I needed some space."

For Christ's sake, I thought to myself, *get a grip and tell him the real reason.* I pushed him away.

"Actually, Aaron," I continued, "I felt like shit in there one minute and the next, I was over aware of everything and everyone around me. My senses were in overdrive and I thought I was going to go mad. I felt ravenous."

"What?" he replied, sobering up instantly, "how do you mean?"

"I want the truth, Aaron," I said, looking deeply into his beautiful eyes, "we need to talk."

"Shit! You're breaking up with me aren't you?"

"I think this is a little more important than whether we're still an item or not, but actually, no – I am not breaking up with you."

"Thank God for that," Aaron said, sighing heavily, "I was starting to worry."

I pulled him down on to the bed so that we were sitting opposite each other.

"I didn't get a transfusion, did I?"

Aaron averted his gaze immediately; his silence alone

was enough to confirm my suspicions.

"Well?" I asked.

"Baby, you lost so much blood, so, so much. They put you into a medically induced coma. I'm so sorry, angel, I should have been there. It should never have got that far; I should have kept my eyes on Jack like a hawk."

Even though I had guessed correctly, I still felt a deep sense of shock. I may have wanted the truth but I wasn't really that prepared for it.

"They wanted to turn off your life support," Aaron went on, "but there was no way I was letting you go. So, you obviously know what happened next."

I nodded; feeling like a weight had been lifted from my shoulders.

"I had to do it – you have to believe me. I'm so sorry. I know it was selfish of me but I don't regret it one bit and I don't know if this helps any, but I didn't give you enough to turn you, not completely. I was careful, I promise."

"Careful?" I shouted, feeling rage flow through me, "Really? Then why is it I could hear blood pumping through the veins of all those people? I felt like I could have fed there and then; luckily I took myself out of the situation."

"Ah, you see, Bea, that's the thing; I only gave you enough to bring you back which means you won't have the same reactions as a *true* vampire."

"Right, so I'm no danger to the community then?" I asked sarcastically.

"Well, no – not at the moment."

"What the hell is that supposed to mean?" I shouted.

"It means that you are not a threat to anyone, yet."

"So, will I become a *true* vampire or am I going to be stuck in this limbo forever?"

"The moment you have to give your blood to another person; then you'll be fully converted." Aaron answered with an awkward smile. His attempt at humour did nothing to brighten my mood, not even slightly.

"So, what you're saying then is that I am essentially a vampire? I mean, I really felt like I could have done something terrible tonight. I don't know what made me run but who's to say I'll run again?"

"Bea, you resisted. Your humanity is obviously strong enough to overpower the urge."

"And that's supposed to make me feel better?" I asked angrily.

"Well, yes and no," Aaron answered, "If you carry on resisting the urge, carry on making a choice, it will just become second nature. It won't be so much of a battle."

I pondered his words for a moment.

"Aaron, I couldn't handle what I was feeling at the gig...."

"You did though. It's why you did the right thing and removed yourself from the situation," Aaron interrupted.

"Yes, I know that but it means from now on, I'm always going to struggle in those situations. I'm supposed to be doing a god damn job here, Aaron! It's going to look totally unprofessional when, one minute I'm shooting and the next, I'm legging it because I'm worried I might kill a gig-goer."

"Oh, Bea," Aaron said, pulling me into his lap and hugging me, "Jim and I have agreed – you need only shoot for as long as you can manage. You'll have free reign which isn't much different to what you have now, is it?"

He had a point.

"I'm scared, Aaron," I said, feeling like I could cry at any second, "what if I lose it?"

"You won't, Bea; I'm sure of it."

"You can't know that; none of us can."

"I'll say it again, honey; you just keep doing what you're doing and you'll get through this. There's no one hundred percent guarantee that you won't *want* or *need* to feed, but you have showed that you *can* resist," Aaron reassured me.

"What happened to them, Aaron - the people I saw you feed on?"

"Well, we can't turn everyone we bite, honey. We tell them the risks but they're so intent that it's hard not to just give in to ourselves and do it. They're fully aware of what might happen. I know that doesn't excuse what we do but I promise you, I rarely feed like that anymore. I do it only when it's absolutely necessary and that's only if we run out of the bags Jim gets from the hospital."

"Blood bags?" I asked, feeling nauseous.

"No, leather bags," Aaron replied, realising quickly that his attempt at lightening the conversation fell on deaf ears, "of course blood bags, what else."

"How did you arrange that then?"

"Let's just say we have a mutual agreement with our local hospital. That's all you need to know."

To be honest, that's really all I *wanted* to know. My brain couldn't handle any more shocks and revelations but I knew that Aaron was telling me nothing but the truth.

Chapter 21

Aaron was sat at the dresser and looked to be writing a note of some sort. I rubbed my eyes and checked the time; eleven forty seven. By anyone's standard, that was a huge lie in but then, it's fair to say I had reason to. I slowly got up out of bed, yawning as I stretched out my limbs and padded over the soft, shag pile to him.

"Hey," I said sleepily.

"Hey, you; someone slept well didn't they? A world war wouldn't have woke you up."

"I was snoring, wasn't I?" I knew I must have been because my mouth felt dry.

"Yes but it was really cute, you know."

Now there was a word I would never have associated with my snoring; sometimes it's that loud that it wakes me. Aaron was obviously just trying to be kind.

"What are you writing?"

"Well, at first I started writing you a note," Aaron answered, "just a quick one to say that I was popping out to get some *proper* coffee. I can't stand the shit you get in hotel rooms. You would think somewhere like this would prioritise good coffee. And that we had missed breakfast. I mean, they only serve between seven and nine. How stupid is that?"

I smiled, nodding in silent agreement.

"But then I got a little waylaid," he went on, "you see, I got this idea for a new song and I had to get it down on paper before I lost it."

"Ooh, can I have a look?" I asked, snatching at the hotel's logo headed paper.

"Hell no!" he shot back.

"Oh, come on, please," I begged.

"Bea, hasn't a rock star ever told you why they don't share their work with *anyone* until they're done with it?"

"Um, no – I don't believe I've ever had the pleasure."

Aaron shook his head, that all too familiar, sexy smirk breaking across his face.

"When will I get to have a look then?" I went on, happily frustrated.

"Who says you'll ever need to?" Aaron replied, "You'll be hearing it soon enough."

"Is it for me; did you write me a song?"

"Maybe," Aaron answered.

"That's a *yes* then?"

"Maybe."

"Jesus Christ, Aaron; stop being a dick."

He laughed out loud, folded the paper and slipped it into his back pocket.

"I bet you're like this at Christmas right?" he asked but went on anyway, not waiting for my answer, "I imagine you just keep going on and on at someone until they break and tell you what your gift is."

I let out a theatrical gasp.

"I can't deny it, I do get a bit excited. Christmas is my favourite time of year."

"And I guess that's because you have so many gifts to

open?"

"Can you tell me anyone who *doesn't* like receiving gifts?" I asked. Aaron couldn't answer that.

"Exactly," I went on.

"So, what's your typical Christmas?" he asked.

I felt my throat start to tighten and my eyes began to brim with tears.

"Oh God," Aaron said, "I'm sorry."

I did nothing to stop the sob that escaped my mouth.

"It's okay," I said, my voice trembling, "don't be silly. It's nothing."

I sank into his chest, breathing in his scent of just-washed clothes and heady, spicy cologne. I didn't want to pull away and I didn't want to talk but I couldn't leave Aaron hanging.

"The good news is, they're not dead," I said, answering a question that hadn't even been asked. I felt Aaron relax his posture. "They separated ten years back, that's all."

"That's all! That's a pretty big deal you know, especially if you're close."

"Well, yeah – I suppose it is really. I'm getting used to it now though, kind of."

Aaron stroked my hair and with each touch, I felt I could give a little more away.

"I mean, it's silly really. I'm a grown woman. I have my own place. I'm completely independent. It hurts though, to think that they'll never be together as a couple again."

"It's not silly at all," Aaron said, "it would be unnatural of you to feel any other way about it."

"So, anyway – Christmas," I continued, "it's the reason I love it so much. For a whole week, I go and stay with my mum and we see my dad most days. Sometimes if he's had a bit too much to drink, after way too much encouragement from me, Mum lets him crash over." I smiled as I thought back to last Christmas; Aaron smiled back.

"I bet that's awkward, right?"

"Well, you'd think so, wouldn't you," I replied, "but actually, they get on better now than they ever did. It's almost like the separation has bought them closer together, even if it's just for a few days."

"Yeah, I get that," Aaron said, nodding, "but you don't see them all year apart from Christmas?"

"Well, I do see them now and again but it really is just fleeting visits and meeting up for dinner on birthdays and stuff. The time they split up was very difficult for each one of us but it gave me the kick up the arse I needed. I took everything in my life for granted up until that point. Together, they did everything for me, possibly even too much so I needed to show them that they didn't have to worry about me on top of all the other stuff they had to sort out as a result of the split. I needed to make my own way; carve my own path."

"Well, you're certainly doing that Bea," Aaron smiled and kissed me, "I think that's why I'm so drawn to you. You're your own person; you don't have to rely on anyone or anything else. That's a very attractive trait."

I quickly washed and as I pulled on my jeans, threw on a light t-shirt, put my boots on, tied a hoodie around my waist (just in case) and ruffled my hands through my hair, I felt my stomach growl with hunger; my confessional had given me a raging appetite, thankfully not for blood. I pulled away from Aaron.

"Anyway, can we continue this over some food – I'm ravenous."

"Sure thing, honey," Aaron said as he pulled me up and out of our room.

Chapter 22

You know those days that you never want to end? That's exactly what I felt when Aaron dropped me back at the hotel.

"So we're on at nine-ish again," he said between soft kisses.

"I know," I sighed.

"No support tonight either."

"What?" I asked, confused. There's *always* a support.

"Yup, dropped out at the last minute," he went on, still kissing, this time peppering them down my neck, "Jim text me while we were at lunch. I didn't say anything though; I didn't want to talk *work*."

"You need a support act, Aaron. People have paid to see you *and* special guests and I know that for the most part, your fans are only interested in seeing you, but that's what's advertised. That's what it says on all the posters and the tickets, right?"

"Yes, I know – you don't have to remind me," he answered, looking frustrated, "I'm sure Jim will try and get something sorted."

"I hope so, honey but it'll be hard finding anyone at short notice."

"Hey, maybe you should be our deputy manager, you obviously know what you're talking about," he said as sweat broke on his brow. I could almost imagine the cogs turning in his head.

"Look," I said, "if the worst comes to the worst, I'll get up and belt out a few numbers." I couldn't stop the snort of laughter that shot out of my mouth. The thought of me being on stage, in front of a couple of thousand people, singing, was quite possibly the funniest thing ever but then I opened my eyes and saw the look on Aaron's face; a serious and hopeful expression. I started to shake my head, silently answering the question he was just about to ask. "No. No way – it was just a joke."

"You do sing though, right?" Aaron asked, "I know you do. I know it's your biggest passion outside of photography and your music writing."

"What the," I said, surprised at just how much he knew about me.

"Don't you know, Bea? A stalker knows everything about who they're stalking. It's a fine art." Aaron laughed and smiled awkwardly.

"I can't remember ever actually mentioning that *anywhere*," I said, smiling back.

"Oh, you so did. New Music; Non Stop - issue one hundred and two. It was the Spotlight on Success interview with the wonderful Beatrice Harvey," he reeled off concisely and it worried me that he remembered far more than I did.

"Wow. What can I say?" I asked after a brief pause in conversation, "You really do know your stuff."

"So?" Aaron said, clasping his hands together and grinning like the Cheshire Cat.

"So?" I asked back.

"C'mon, Bea, please. I know you can do this. Do it for me, I beg you."

"That's not begging now, is it," I said, wondering why the hell I was even answering Aaron, let alone contemplating what he was asking, "If you *really* want me to do it, you've got to do way better than that; on your knees Aaron Holmes."

"Seriously?" he asked.

"Seriously," I replied, holding back a snigger of amusement, "now kneel."

Aaron looked at me, shaking his head as he realised just how deadly serious I was being. I felt powerful and I loved it. He slowly dropped to his knees and looked up at me. All I could think about was what I could do to him; he looked so damn sexy. He must have picked up on the atmosphere as he flashed that smirk at me and I very nearly turned to jelly right in front of him.

"Beatrice Harvey – please, please, *please* would you support Shout the Call tonight?"

I stared blankly out of the window. I wasn't about to agree to anything just yet. He needed to work just that little bit extra.

"Please, Bea, I beg you. Look at me," he said; this time really laying it on thick, "I'm on my knees and everything. Please."

"You may stand," I replied.

"Does that mean you will?"

"It means you can get up off your knees."

"Bloody hell, Bea."

"Now, now; that kind of language isn't going to help your cause, my dear." I said and it took every fibre of my being to stop the belly laugh that was threatening to erupt.

"Shit, I'm sorry, but come on," he said, wound up like a coil, "just answer, please."

"Hmm," I replied, rubbing my chin in faux contemplation, "well I suppose you have begged and pleaded quite well, so."

Aaron clapped his hands and jumped up and down like an over excited child at Christmas.

"Um, I haven't answered you yet," I continued, drawing things out even more. He stopped his little jig immediately; he looked drained. I dragged on the silence as long as I comfortably could.

"Okay."

"Okay as in *yes*?" he asked; a pained expression playing on his face.

"Yes, I suppose I can help you out – just this once."

Aaron's arms enveloped me as he squeezed me tightly, showering kisses all over my face.

"Thank you, thank you, thank you," he chirruped

between even more kisses, "you will not regret this."

******

"Shit!" Aaron shouted as he punched a hole in the headboard before covering his mouth; his fangs must have been out. "I'm sorry, honey."

"Don't be upset," I said, sitting upright and taking his face in my hands, "I'm not. I think it's pretty amazing that I turn you on so much. Damn it; that's such an arrogant thing to say. I didn't mean it like that. I meant," I trailed off as the proverbial hole I was doing a good job of digging, got deeper and deeper.

"Hey," he stopped me, "no apology required. You're completely right – you seriously turn me on."

I pulled him into a deep hug and kissed his cheek.

"Anyway, changing the subject slightly; exactly what am I going to be singing tonight?"

"Just go with about five of your favourite songs. No slow tracks though; they've got to be fast and frantic; rocking, you know? Anything close to our sound and you're there."

"Okay," I gulped, feeling the nerves really settling in.

"And you don't have to worry about whether the band know the songs or not" he went on, "they all started as session musicians. You won't believe the stuff they know off the top of their heads. Just choose your songs and I'll let them know. If there's anything they don't know, then we'll just pick something else."

I shook my head, fully coming to terms with what I had agreed to.

"Now let's get you ready," he went on, "we haven't got long until sound check."

I felt a wave of nervous nausea wash over me.

******

If it wasn't for the fact that the crowd lapped up ever single second of Beatrice & The Harvey's set, I probably would have fallen in the first few bars of the first song. As my time on stage came to an end, I looked around at Tim, Alex, Liam and Jack who were smiling unabashedly at me. I smiled back. I had just performed my first, proper gig. I felt utter elation as the crowd chanted for more. The schedule was tight though, so after I thanked the band, the crowd and, last but not least, Aaron, I headed off stage. Aaron stood at the base of the steps that led down to the corridor with a gigantic smile on his face. I smiled back, still half in shock. He pulled me into his chest and hugged me tighter than he had ever done before.

"Jesus Christ, Bea – that was unbelievable. I just, well, oh man, it was awesome." His words tumbled over themselves.

"Thank you," I replied, not caring much for the sweat dripping from my hair on to his shoulders.

"No, seriously – thank you, honey. You've saved our bacon tonight and you've given me yet another reason to utterly adore you."

I felt a shiver run through me; he could not have said anything better.

"Thank you, again. Thank you for believing in me. Thank you for giving me this opportunity. If I never get up on a stage again, I'm happy. That was amazing. I've done little gigs here and there in the past but this is in a whole different league. It's going to take a while to come down from this."

"And you could totally see that," Aaron said excitedly, "you owned it, honey – one hundred per cent."

I blushed.

"Hey," he went on, pushing me away gently, still holding my waist, "why don't you get cleaned up and grab a few drinks while we're on. Enjoy the set and then I'll catch up with you afterwards. I've got a little surprise up my sleeve. You're going to love it."

I grinned from ear to ear as Aaron turned me round and slapped my backside playfully before he headed off down the corridor.

******

It may have been because I was still on an all time high from performing, it may have been that the drinks were going down far too well but Shout the Call looked and sounded better than I had ever heard them. Everything felt perfect and if there was a bottle in existence big enough, I would have poured the atmosphere in and shoved the cork in tight.

The band blasted out their encore and I took this as my cue to retreat backstage. I couldn't wait to see Aaron and whatever this surprise was. I grabbed a beer from the fridge in our dressing room and plonked down on one of the settees. I took a long, deep gulp and shivered; the freezing cold temperature taking itself out on my teeth and my head. Aaron came bounding into the room.

"Hey," he said, running up and practically throwing himself at me before kissing me hard on the lips, "so how's my multi-talented, gorgeous girlfriend?"

"She's very well thank you," I answered, "still buzzing actually."

"Good good," he said, smiling widely and rubbing his hands together, "and is she ready for her surprise?"

He headed towards the door and opened it, just slightly, not even waiting for my answer.

"You can come in now," he said, out into the corridor. I fidgeted with anticipation and then my mouth dropped open in amazement before it stretched into a wide smile.

Chapter 23

"Dad! Oh my God," I shouted as I ran into my father's open arms, instantly feeling like a little girl again as I buried my face into his jumper.

"Beatrice," he said, choking back tears, "how are you my darling?"

"I'm great, Dad, just great. I can't believe you're here. I've missed you and Mum so much. What's bought you here? Where's Mum? Are you okay?"

"Slow down, sweetheart," he replied, laughing.

"Sorry, Dad, I'm just so happy to see you."

"I know - me too. We both miss you very much."

"Could Mum not come, then?"

"She's off on conference duties in Italy," he answered apologetically, "she couldn't get out of it I'm afraid. She has sent this though."

My father practically skipped out of the room. He reappeared with a neat, perfectly wrapped present in his hand and offered it out to me. I shook my head.

"She really didn't need to buy me anything."

"She knows that, Beatrice but between you and me, I know how much she's missing you so this is the next best thing."

I turned the gift over and over in my hands, trying to guess its contents. It was square and soft. *It's a jumper* I thought to myself. I opened the package, almost frantically, to find a lovely pair of plaid, fleece pj's which is exactly what I needed for those cool nights on the bus.

"And here's a little something from me," he went on, "it's not much but I hope you like it." He pulled another gift out of his back pocket. It was a slim, rectangular black case. I opened it to find a beautiful new fountain pen.

"Oh, Dad," I said, rolling the pen between the thumb and index finger of my right hand, "It's just perfect; beautiful. You really shouldn't have, neither of you needed to but thank you so much." I hugged my father again.

"Anyway," I went on, "you never answered my question. What are you doing here? I mean that in the nicest possible way."

"Wait, so I need a reason to come and see my favourite daughter?"

"*Favourite* daughter eh?" I asked as I looked up at his face, grinning, "Are you telling me you've got a love child or maybe more out there?"

He laughed heartily. "Yes, Beatrice, there's a load of them knocking around."

I laughed back.

"Dad, seriously – how many times? It's Bea. I always feel like I'm in trouble or something when you use my full name."

"Okay, if you insist, Beatrice," he replied, "oops, sorry, Bea. I can't help it – you're still my little girl," he said as he bought his right hand up to my face and pinched my cheek playfully.

"Actually, there is a reason I wanted to come and see you," he continued, turning serious.

"What's the matter, Dad? What's wrong?"

"Oh, my darling, everything's fine, it's just….."

"Dad, spit it out!"

"Look, let me take you out for coffee and cake just like we used to," he said with a smile.

Actually, that did sound pretty good. I'm sure I saw an *open-all-hours* diner on the way here in the taxi. I looked at Aaron.

"Is that okay?"

"Of course! Go and have some time with your dad and I'll see you back at the room later," he replied and kissed my forehead, "Goodbye, Mr Harvey, it was lovely meeting you."

"Goodbye, Aaron – you too."

******

There's been a big craze over these American style diners for heaven knows how long now around our parts, and it had obviously caught on here too, but I had never been in one, until now. It was as clichéd as I expected; waitresses on roller skates and stripy, 1950's style, pinafore dresses. Their hair and make up was pristine and it made me realise that I really needed to make more of an effort with my appearance – I didn't look that good on a night out.

"What would you like, sweetheart?" Dad asked without looking up, flicking through his own menu and looking bewildered.

"I'll have a filter coffee, none of that decaf malarkey though, and a slice of carrot cake please," I said to our waitress, who I couldn't take my eyes off. She was stunning - too stunning to be working in a glorified café anyway, if you ask me.

Dad was shaking his head in confusion.

"There's just so much and it all sounds delicious," he said.

"I can come back in a little while, Sir," The waitress offered in the best English I had heard in the little while we'd been in the country.

"Dad," I shot in, "I thought we were just going to have coffee and cake, *like we used to?*"

That put him right straight away.

"Of course, you're right," he went on, "I'll have the same as my daughter please."

"Coming right up," she said with a wink.

The carrot cake was delicious and moist and actually, pretty light compared to some others I've had. It was clear we were enjoying our sweet treats because neither of us uttered a word while we ate but there were more than a few noises of appreciation escaping our mouths.

"Well, that wasn't nice at all," Dad said sarcastically as he wiped his mouth with a napkin and pointed to a solitary crumb on his plate..

"I think that was quite possibly the nicest cake ever and this coffee is perfect," I said as I savoured the mixture of flavours in my mouth.

"It really is," Dad agreed.

Suddenly, an awkward, uncomfortable and somewhat inevitable silence nestled itself in between us.

"So, come on, Dad, let's talk."

Dad sighed and his shoulders dropped.

"Now, don't panic, darling, and please try not to get upset, okay?"

I started to panic and got upset immediately. What did he expect when he asks questions like that?

"Okay, fine. Hit me with it!"

"I'm not very well, sweetheart."

"How *not well*?" I asked, feeling the pit of my stomach drop, "You obviously haven't come all this way to tell me you have a cold."

"I sincerely wish that was the case, Beatrice."

"Same here, Dad," I said, mentally preparing myself for what was to come.

My dad called our waitress over. I looked straight at him in disbelief and I couldn't quite believe he was interrupting our serious talk by ordering something else.

"Are you still serving alcohol, dear?" he asked her.

"Yes we are – everything's 24 hours here, Sir," she replied with a sugary sweet smile.

"What's your top brand whiskey please?"

"We have *Chivas Regal* or *Famous Grouse.*"

"Make it two doubles of the first then please, young lady."

"Look, Beatrice," my father said after our whiskeys had been delivered to our table, "last thing I wanted to do was come here and tell you this, sweetheart. I really wish I was here, with you, just for the fun of it; to see you doing what you love. Hanley's already told me how well you're doing in the company and when he told me you got this gig, I was thrilled. I'm over the moon for you, Beatrice. I know how much it means to you; I know how much you love this band."

I could feel tears welling up in my eyes. I took a large gulp of the stinging liquid and struggled to get it past the lump in my throat. I couldn't utter a word for fear of breaking down and it was obvious my dad was struggling too.

"Don't cry, Beatrice, please don't."

"I'm sorry, Dad, I can't help it."

My father gulped down the rest of his whiskey in one hit. He winced. "Honey, I have cancer."

I looked at him in complete disbelief but at the same time, I knew he wasn't lying – not about something as serious as this.

"Can it be treated? Is it curable? What type is it?" I fired off quickly. I didn't want the words lingering in my mouth; I wanted the questions out of my head.

"I'm so sorry, sweetheart but it's terminal bowel cancer. It was simply found too late to cure. Anyway," he said, pausing to give us both a bit of respite, "I phoned Hanley and he told me you were here. I explained everything and he gave me Jim's number. I ordered Hanley not to speak a word of this to anyone; he promised me. He's clearly very good at keeping his promises. Then

I phoned Jim and asked if it was possible to catch up with you on the tour and well, here I am. You understand why I couldn't tell you something like this over the phone, right?"

"Yes, I understand," I said, still in shock.

"Would you have come on this tour if I told you four weeks ago, when I originally found out?"

"What the hell? You should have said something, Dad, and no, you know I couldn't have."

"You see, there you go," he said almost smugly, "there was no way on this earth I would have ruined this opportunity for you."

I broke down into deep, heavy sobs; I couldn't hold it in any more. I felt like I had been slapped, hard, across the face. Truth is, I knew Dad hadn't been too well for quite some time but I hadn't any idea as to what extent.

"You're not saying goodbye now are you? You can't. Not yet; no way."

"Beatrice, I'm afraid I can't defy the inevitable. The good news is…."

"Good news? Are you having a laugh?" I shot at him.

"The good news is," my father continued, "I'll be joining you for a few days, health permitting. I won't be on the bus with you but I'll be following your movements. Oh dear, that sounds creepy doesn't it? Hanley's already arranged accommodation for me for the next few nights and then we'll just have to see how things go. Don't worry; I won't be hovering around, cramping your style. I'll just be around if you need me."

I zoned out, my father's words sounding like a distant murmur and my thoughts turned to my grandparents. They meant the world to me. My Grandmother knew me better than I knew myself and to my Grandfather, I was an angel. I could do no wrong. I never entertained the idea that some day, they would be gone. They were a strong constant in my life. They were both diagnosed with dementia as well as other health problems but it was dementia that sparked the beginning of the end. I remember how they had their good days and their very bad days. On the good days, it was as if they had regressed ten or so years and the conversation was rich and wonderful. On the bad days, they hadn't a clue who I was and they believed my parents were evil. A few days before they each passed, I distinctly remember them perking up. I clearly recall having coherent, lovely chats with them. It was the best time I'd had with either of them for what felt like forever. It was as if they were trying to let me know that they would be fine. That none of us had to worry. I have no real understanding of cancer at all but I understood immediately that my father was here to let me know exactly what my grandparents had done years before him - it's going to be okay.

"Oh, Dad, I just don't know what to say," I sighed deeply.

"I know, Beatrice," he said, stroking my arm, "anyway; I'm going to head off now. I want to try and beat you to Denmark."

"How are you getting there, Dad?"

"I'm booked in on a ferry tonight and then I'll just use public transport to get me to the hotel."

"Oh, okay. Well please make sure you phone me as soon as you hit Denmark. I don't care what time it is, just let me know you're there safe."

"Of course I will, sweetheart, and maybe we can go for lunch – you know, some *real* food."

"Yes, that would be great. I was just going to suggest the same. It's a date."

"Come on, let's get you back to your rock-star boyfriend," he said, gesturing to the waitress for our bill.

Chapter 24

"Goodnight, sweetheart," Dad said as he hugged me tight in the hotel's reception, "I'll see you soon, okay? Enjoy what's left of your night, or should I say, morning."

My eyes filled with tears again as I watched him walk away and wave goodbye. *What if that's the last I ever see of my dad?* I thought to myself. I shook my head as if the aggressive action would remove it from my brain.

I got in the lift and made my way straight to our room. I slipped my key card in the slot and opened the door. Aaron got up from the bed, chewing at his nails. He walked right up to me and pulled me into his arms.

"Hey, honey, you okay?"

I'd almost completely forgotten that he hadn't been

with me and as much as I really didn't want to replay it all over again, he needed to know and I needed to pour my heart and soul out to him.

"It's cancer," I answered simply, "he has cancer."

"Shit!"

"Yes."

"Can they treat it?" he asked and all I could do was shake my head; I couldn't say it out loud.

"Oh, Bea," he went on, "I don't know what to say. I'm so, so sorry."

"It's okay," I said, pulling at his black knitted jumper and pressing my face to this chest. I couldn't stop my breath catching as I broke into tears again.

"Let it all out, honey," he whispered into my hair, "let it all go."

******

"What time is it?" I practically bellowed as I woke up and realised I had forgotten to set my alarm.

"It's okay, Bea, it's only seven," Aaron assured, "we

don't have to leave for another hour and a half. Here, I bought you coffee."

The coffee tasted so good as it flowed down my throat.

"What time did I finally drift off?"

"About three, honey, well thereabouts anyway."

"And, you've been awake all that time, haven't you?" I asked, knowing how shitty I feel when deprived of sleep.

"It's fine, us vampires don't have to worry about sleep."

Of course, I thought to myself, *how could I forget?*

There was a rapping at the door.

"Who is it?" Aaron called out as I was busy putting the finishing touches to my make-up and hair.

"It's me, mate," Jim's muffled reply came through the door, "can I come in?"

"Yeah, yeah – hang on," Aaron answered as he got up from the bed and opened the door.

"You guys almost ready?" Jim asked.

"Yes," I answered and turned to face him. I'm sure my mascara hadn't run – I'd only just put it on but Jim looked at me and I knew he sensed there was something wrong.

"You okay there, Bea?" he asked sympathetically, "you look a bit glum."

"I'll talk to you later, mate," Aaron shot in which thankfully gave me a chance to take a deep breath and compose myself.

"Okey dokey," he said, still looking straight at me, "well, it was just to say that you need to be out front in fifteen minutes okay?"

"Yup," Aaron answered for us both again, "see you in a bit."

******

Much to Aaron's mild annoyance, I didn't manage a wink of sleep on the bus. He kept asking me to try but I was restlessly tired – the worst kind of tired to be. My head swam with thoughts on how and when I would have to say goodbye to my dad. Would I write a eulogy for his funeral? Would I read it? How would my Mom react? Would her heart break too?

After what felt like an eternity, we finally got into

Denmark. We parked up outside Train, one of Denmark's top music venues according to the brief introduction Jim had given, on *Toldbodgade 6*.

It was an amazing venue, reminding me a lot of the Astoria in London. Such a terrible shame that place closed. It's such a loss to the scene. I wandered off on my own for a little while, taking it all in. I made my way up into the balcony and sat down right in the middle of the front row. I could see the photo pit and knew it was going to be snug to say the least. I never heard Jim approach behind me. I was away in my own world.

"Bea, I've spoke to Aaron," he said, putting his hand on my shoulder as he took a seat next to me, "I'm so sorry about your dad, sweet. How are you coping? Wait, stupid question, um...."

I put my hand on Jim's knee.

"It's okay, Jim," I answered, "I'm fine, honestly. Well, no, I'm not fine but well, what can I do?"

"You can take another night off, that's what. You're not working tonight," he said, pulling me into a warm, fatherly hug, "honestly, Bea, take as long as you need."

I shot Jim a look that implied I would do no such thing. I had already taken too much time off, and anyway, I needed to get back on it as much for my own sanity than doing what I was being paid for.

"Jim, honestly – it's fine. I'm cool," I said even though it was clear I wasn't, "anyway, I have all day to meet up with my dad. Actually, we've already arranged a catch up. I just have to find out where and when he wants to meet."

"As long as you're absolutely sure, Bea," Jim replied sympathetically, "We would completely understand."

"I know, Jim," I whispered, hugging him tightly, "anyway, I'm getting withdrawal symptoms already – I need my Shout the Call fix."

"Right," he said, "well, I've got to go and meet the manager and the sound tech, so I'll leave you to it. You okay on your own?"

I nodded and kissed Jim's cheek.

******

I headed to the bar and caught the barmaid just before she opened the door to what I imagine was a staff room. It was clear her shift wasn't about to start any time soon; her head bobbing to whatever music was coming through her headphones and chewing on a long strawberry lace which hung from her lips.

"Any chance?" I asked.

"Well, I'm not really supposed to....." she trailed off, obviously wanting to get away. I put on my best little-girl-lost impression.

"Come on, pretty please?" I asked again, "I could really do with a drink right now."

Barmaid looked around nervously.

"Shit, okay," she answered anxiously, "just don't tell anyone, right?"

"My lips are sealed."

"So, what's your poison?" she asked quietly.

"I think maybe the question should be *what isn't*?" I laughed before pondering over what to have, "Make it a Jack Daniel's. Please."

"On the rocks?"

"Of course."

"Single or double?"

That was easy enough to answer, "Double please."

She poured my drink and pushed it across the bar in front of me. I took a deep breath, exhaled, picked up the glass and downed its contents in one.

"Whoa," I winced, "same again please."

After throwing back a fourth double measure of bourbon, I heard Aaron behind me.

"Honey, you carry on drinking like that and the only thing you'll be meeting is the floor," he said softly as he pulled up a bar stool and sat next to me. I looked at the four empty glasses lined up in front of me and felt pretty disgusted.

"Shit!" I said, shocked I'd got as far as I had.

"Yup – someone's going for it eh?"

"I didn't mean to, I mean, I can't believe it." I stuttered, ashamed of myself.

"Hey, don't get yourself worked up over it, Bea – it's pretty understandable considering. You just need to choose; drink yourself into oblivion or don't and go off to meet your Dad."

Of course, there was no way in the world I was going to miss meeting him. No. Way.

"Would you like another?" Barmaid asked, "it's just I really shouldn't be doing this. I don't start until later."

"No. No, thank you – no more."

"Good girl," Aaron said, smiling warmly at me, "do

you know where you're meeting?"

"Not yet, I still have to phone him."

"Well, what are you waiting for – give him a ring. I'll walk you to wherever you decide to meet, you know, just to make sure you get there safe. Sound cool?"

"Thank you," I said, turning to face him full on, kissing him tenderly. I pulled my phone out of my pocket, found my father's number and hit dial.

"It's just ringing out then going to voicemail," I barked at Aaron, starting to worry that after six attempts to call, my dad still wasn't answering.

"He might just be getting ready," he replied looking totally unconvinced by the words spilling from his mouth.

"Or he might," I said to myself as much to Aaron, "He might have collapsed. He might have...."

Aaron put his hands on my shoulders and gripped them firmly. I almost expected him to shake me; to tell me not to be so silly.

"Look, Bea, let's just calm down huh? We don't know anything until we've seen him. Let me speak to Jim. I'll ask him if he knows where your dad is staying. If he's not sure, Hanley will be."

He pulled his phone out and put it to his ear, walking

to the other side of the room which was probably for the best – I was close to having a full blown panic attack. *Breathe*, I told myself; *just breathe.*

After what felt like an age, even though he had only been on the phone a couple of minutes, Aaron headed back over to me looking more than a little accomplished.

"He's at the *Hotel Royal*. Now, I don't know where the hell that is so Jim's going to come with us in the taxi he's just booked."

I threw my arms around him and didn't even try to stop the tears pouring from my eyes.

"Hey hey hey," Aaron said, stroking my back, "let's try and stay positive okay?"

He was right, of course, but I just had this horrible feeling deep down in my gut.

Chapter 25

The ride to the *Royal Hotel* was silent and I managed to bite every fingernail right down to the quick. I felt sick to my stomach and didn't dare to speak for fear of breaking down, again.

We pulled up outside the hotel and I could have smashed the window just to get out but Aaron, once again, knew how to soothe me.

"Shh," he said, stroking my hair, "you need to calm down and take a long, deep breath. Your dad won't want to see you in a state."

"You think he's dying, don't you?"

"I don't think *anything* yet, honey," he answered firmly, "let's just see what's going on."

I nodded and attempted a smile. Aaron scooped up my right hand and pulled me towards the entrance of the huge, grand, looming building in front of us.

"We're looking for Mr. Harvey," Aaron said, not even saying a polite hello to the girl on reception.

"Paul Harvey," I added.

"And who is asking?" she replied.

"I'm his daughter, Beatrice. Beatrice Harvey. This is my boyfriend, Aaron," I replied.

Girl-on-Reception looked Aaron up and down suggestively, utterly blanking my response, opting instead to converse only with my boyfriend.

"Do I know you, Sir?" she asked. It was pretty obvious that she did as she stood there curling her hair round her fingers.

"Quite possibly; I'm lead singer in a band called Shout the Call," Aaron answered, "but, and excuse my rudeness, I'm not here to discuss me. We've told you why we're here so can you help us please?"

The flirting quickly fizzled out and the look on her face was priceless. Her eyes dropped to the computer monitor in front of her and she tapped away on the keys.

"Mr. Harvey is staying in room twenty three on the

second floor. Would you like me to request he come down?"

"Actually, we need to go up to see him."

"Well, it's not company policy......"

"Look, screw your damn policy," Aaron shot in, becoming more exasperated by the second – now who needed to calm down? "The guy's not well and we're not sure if he has the strength to come down. Beatrice was supposed to be meeting up with him today but she hasn't been able to get hold of him to arrange where. So, can you please let us up to him?"

"I suppose...." she said, mulling over the question.

"Come on," Aaron almost shouted, "please, we need to see him; we have to."

"Okay, okay – go on up," she said, handing Aaron a key card, "I'm going to get in so much trouble over this!"

"Thank , Miss," Aaron said to her, grabbing my hand and pulling me towards the stairs "and don't worry, if anyone ever does find out, I promise I'll cover for you."

We came to a sharp halt outside room twenty three.

"I can't do this, Aaron."

"Yes you can," he said, his eyes full of sympathy,

"you must."

"I'm scared. What if….."

"I know you are, honey and that's completely natural. Deep breath, okay?"

I inhaled on cue and with shaking hands, I knocked on the door. No answer. "Dad," I called; still no answer. Aaron slipped the key card from his back pocket and pushed it into the slot above the door handle. A green light flashed and I slammed the door open.

"Dad," I shouted, running over to my father, lying unconscious on the king size bed, "oh my God. Dad!"

I grabbed his chin in my right hand and shook his head sharply from side to side. His eyes stayed shut so I shook even harder. "Daddy," I yelled, hoping the increase in volume would have more of an effect. His eyes slowly flickered open.

"Dad, it's me."

"Beatrice," he whispered hoarsely, "oh my darling. I'm so sorry I couldn't meet up with you…"

"Shush," I stopped him, "it's okay; I'm here now."

He looked towards Aaron who was still standing at the door, and smiled weakly.

"How did you know I was here?" he asked.

"Let's just say Aaron's been my private investigator," I replied, trying to sound as light hearted as I possibly could. Aaron smiled awkwardly as we both looked at him.

"I just spoke to Jim, that's all," he said quietly.

"Thank you," my dad whispered, smiling at Aaron.

"No problem," Aaron said quietly, looking at his feet.

"So, how are you feeling, Dad?" I asked, immediately feeling foolish; what a stupid question.

"Ah well, you know...."

"No, I don't – tell me."

"Beatrice, there's no easy way of saying this but I think this might be it - I think I'm dying."

"Please, Dad," I said, struggling to swallow the lump in my throat, "don't talk like that."

"Oh, sweetheart, I know but I'm afraid it's the truth."

I looked at Aaron, hoping he would come to sit next to me. He answered my silent plea and headed over to the bed, sat down next to me and began stroking my back.

"We need to get you to a hospital, Dad."

"No point, sweetheart."

"Well, there could be a chance...."

"What chance, sweetheart? It's incurable. Nothing they can do now. I'm happy, Beatrice," he smiled, "You're here, my beautiful daughter. Please don't take me to hospital. Let's stay here, just like this."

We both started to cry.

Aaron's silence was deafening.

"Have you spoken to Mum?" I eked out between sobs.

"No."

"Oh, Dad, why?"

"I won't ruin this conference she's on. It's too important for her. And anyway, as much as it pains me to say this, we're not together anymore."

"Don't you think she needs to know?" I asked again.

"Of course she does," Dad answered quietly, "she already knows I'm terminal. If this is *it*, if this *is* the end, I need you to speak to her when I'm gone."

The deep, intense sadness I felt quickly turned to anger.

"Oh, so it's left to me to do your dirty work. Dad, how the hell do you think that makes me feel?"

"I'm so sorry, but yes," he wheezed before letting out a wracking cough, "I am not prepared to ruin her career."

I could actually see his point even though I didn't particularly like it.

"I'm tired, so tired," he whispered, "Let me just rest my eyes, please?"

"No, Dad," I pleaded, "you do that and you won't come back, will you?"

"I don't know," he answered weakly, "I just need to sleep."

Aaron gently tugged at my right arm.

"Honey, just let him rest. We'll speak to him more when he wakes up."

"If he wakes up!" I whispered.

"Let's just see huh?"

"Okay," I gave in, "but what do we do in the meantime?"

"Hotel bar?"

"Are you serious?" I asked, knowing that he was right

and as much as this angered me, maybe a stiff drink would calm me, if only for a little while.

******

"What do I do, Aaron?" I asked, wincing as I knocked back a double Scotch and making a mental decision to nurse the next one.

"I know this sounds completely and utterly insensitive of me but, about what?" He said sheepishly, "Telling your mum? Taking him to hospital?"

"Well, both, I suppose," I replied as Aaron waved his hand at the guy behind the bar, gesturing for another drink.

"Look, I know you only want the very best for your dad," Aaron said as two more doubles were put in front of us, "and I wouldn't expect anything less from you, but you know something, you'll regret it if you get him into hospital and he slips away in a place he really doesn't want to be."

"I know. I know that but maybe they can just make him more comfortable."

"Look, Bea," he said, taking a sip of his drink, "put yourself in his shoes. Where would you rather be if you had the choice?"

I nodded weakly, Aaron was totally and utterly right.

"And your mum," he continued, "I actually think he's bang on there too. When is her conference exactly?"

"When I spoke to her a couple of days before I came out on tour with you, she said she had a full week and then a presentation at the end of it. She should be on the last leg now."

"Well, this is what I think," he said firmly, "Let's get through tonight. We'll speak to the Manager of the hotel and explain the situation and see if we can stay in the room with your dad, or at the very least, a room close to him anyhow."

"But you have a gig tonight," I said, "you can't cancel."

"We won't be, don't worry," he assured me. I took a calming sip of my drink, "but I'll come back straight after. I won't let you go through this on your own, honey, I promise. You'll just have to bear with me for a little while, okay?"

I nodded and I could feel tears in my eyes again but they weren't for my dad, they were for Aaron – the man I was coming to realise I probably couldn't imagine life without. I felt safe and secure with him. I felt loved.

Aaron had used his charms and arranged it so that we could actually stay in with my dad. The room was more than big enough to get another bed into.

I checked my dad, relieved he was actually *sleeping*. His breathing was a little laboured and shallow but he *was* breathing. For now, that was good enough.

"Honey, I have to go now," Aaron said, walking over to me and kissing me deeply, "you'll be okay, won't you?"

"Yes, honestly – I'll be fine," I answered, hoping he would believe my white lie.

"If you need me for anything, just call Jim. If it's urgent, he'll pull me out and I'll be here as quick as I can."

"I'm sure it won't come to that but I promise I will if it does."

He kissed me again, turned his back and left.

******

I must have drifted off to sleep because I found myself lying on the bed, fully clothed, with Aaron sitting beside me, smiling.

"How long have you been back?" I asked.

"About twenty minutes."

I shot upright, realising I had totally neglected my vigil for my dad.

"Shit! I can't believe I thought it would be okay to just doze off. What if?"

"Relax, honey, its fine," Aaron replied, "I checked him as soon as I got through that door. No change – he's still the same as when I left."

"I know, but I….."

"But, nothing," Aaron said, pulling me back down on to the bed, lying next to and facing me, "you need to be alert to look after your dad. Do you feel better for having a sleep? Do you feel refreshed?"

I knew I must have slept deeply because I never heard or sensed Aaron in the room.

"Yes, I do."

"Well, there you go. Have you eaten yet?"

"Not a scrap," I replied, suddenly feeling my stomach growl.

Aaron picked up the phone on the bedside table and

phoned room service. He ordered enough food to feed the five thousand. I was salivating just listening to him.

******

"Room service," a male voice called out from beyond the door.

"Man, that was quick," Aaron said as he got up and walked to the door, rubbing his hands together.

A trolley full of pizza, fries and assorted salad was pushed into the room and even though the mini bar hadn't been touched, Aaron had ordered a six pack.

"Oh my God," I mumbled through a mouthful of pizza, "this is like heaven. It's better than…."

"Don't even," he said as he stuffed a handful of fries into his mouth, "how can you compare that to a shed load of fast food? There's no contest for me – I'll take a bit of how's-your-father over food any day of the week!"

"Sorry," I giggled, "I was just saying it's so good but don't you worry, I know what I would rather have too!" I winked suggestively at him, forgetting all about the situation we were in. "Anyway, I didn't think vampires fed on or enjoyed anything other than blood?"

"Ah, you see – something else you didn't know," he said, smacking his lips, "like I've already said, senses become heightened when you're a vampire and even though we *need* blood to survive, we still like *normal* food."

"So, the other night, at the gig...." I said, pulling the slice of pizza away from my lips and mentally putting two and two together.

"Yes. Correct."

"So you lied to me then?"

"No. I would never lie to you about that, Bea. You are not a full vampire but you have my blood inside of you which means you will pick up some, maybe even all, of my traits."

"That explains so much."

"I hope so," he said, cracking the tops off two bottles of beer and handing me one. He put his to his lips and gulped. I did the same with mine, "anyway, hurry up with your food okay, I'm hungry for something else."

"Is that a chat-up line?" I laughed, spitting beer all over me.

"Do you want it to be?"

I laughed again but this time, the sound was muffled

by Aaron's mouth on mine. He took my beer and pushed it on to the bedside table and I let him push me backwards on to the soft, downy bed sheets.

He kissed deeply and I kissed back. He pushed my arms up so that they were above my head and pressed them into the pillow. Kisses were trailed down the insides of my arms, one after the other. He nuzzled into my neck, paying attention to both sides and nibbling at my ears. It didn't take long to get far too carried away.

"Stop," I heaved, "Stop. I can't do this with my dad in here. It's completely wrong."

"Oh my God, Bea, I'm so sorry," he said breathlessly, "I just didn't think. I, I just totally forgot."

"It's okay, honey, its okay. So did I!"

"Shush," Aaron said, putting a finger to my lips, "listen."

I couldn't hear a thing apart from my heart racing.

"What am I listening for?"

"Just listen."

And then there was another sound.

My dad was waking up. I could hear his breathing changing - he was definitely coming to. I rushed over to his bedside and waited, holding my own breath just so I could hear his more clear inhalations and exhalations.

"Dad," I whispered, "Dad, it's me. I'm here."

"Mmmm," was the only sound that came from him.

"It's okay. Just take your time."

His eyes slowly opened and he immediately squeezed them shut. I switched off his bedside lamp and gestured to Aaron to switch ours on. He opened them again and this time, his lids stayed put. He looked straight at me and smiled.

"Beatrice," he croaked, "oh my Beatrice."

I stroked his forehead and his cheeks, as tears trickled down my own.

"I'm right here, Dad," I assured him, "How are you feeling?"

"You won't believe me, but I feel," he paused, "okay."

He smiled at me. I smiled back.

"Do you want a drink of water, Dad?"

"Yes, that would be lovely."

I went through to the en suite bathroom, turned over

the tumbler glass that was sitting on the side of the sink and filled it with water. I took it back through to my dad.

"Can you sit up?" I asked him.

He nodded lightly and pushed himself up so he was propped up against the bed's headboard.

"There aren't any straws or anything, Dad, do you think you can manage?"

"We'll soon see," he said as he guided the glass, with my hands still round it, to his mouth. He took a small sip at first and then a substantial gulp. Without warning, to either of us, he rolled on to his side and heaved.

Blood shot from his mouth on to the crisp, white pillow. I leaned over him and rubbed his back, knowing that it really wasn't helping matters.

"Bea, can I have a quick word?" Aaron asked. I turned and looked at him angrily.

"Now?"

"Yes. Now," he answered.

"I don't believe you, Aaron. Look at him," I said, pointing at my dad, who was getting worse by the second.

He grabbed me around the waist and whispered in my ear. "I need to speak to you *now*!"

At that precise moment, it wouldn't have bothered me if I never saw Aaron again but his powers of persuasion are second to none. I cursed under my breath and got up, making it absolutely clear that I was not happy in the slightest.

"This better be phenomenal!" I seethed.

"Beatrice, this is it – he's going," he said, shaking his head.

"No shit!" I shouted at him.

"We can help him you know. There is another way."

"What, digging his grave for him?"

"Hear me out, okay?" Aaron answered.

"Go on then, if you must."

"I can give him my blood." Aaron said; waiting for my reaction which he probably knew wouldn't be a good one.

"What?" I shouted.

"I can make him immortal. He'll never know illness again; he will always be well."

"Well, yippee," I said sarcastically, outraged by his solution, "he'll get rid of his cancer but will have a penchant for sucking blood. Nice. Brilliant idea, Aaron!"

"That's the only way to save him, honey," he replied, "but it's up to you."

"Don't you think it's a decision only my dad can make?"

"Bea, just look at him," Aaron turned my head so I was facing back towards my dad. He was writhing around, his face contorted with pain, blood caked on his lips.

"He's barely here with us," Aaron went on, "and even if he was capable enough to make the decision himself, you know he would hate the thought of it."

He was, even though it pained me to say it, correct. I began to cry again as a deep sense of realisation set in.

"I know. I know. What do I do? What would you do?" I asked.

"You know I can't tell you what to do. It can only be your decision, but if it helps any, if it was me lying before you on the verge of death, I would choose immortality any day of the week. I would never ever want to be away from you. I know it's easier said than done because I'm immortal already but that would be my choice."

I wrapped my arms around him and kissed him deeply.

"I want to save him," I whispered breathlessly into his mouth, tears tumbling down my cheeks.

"Are you sure, Bea?" he whispered back.

"I'm certain."

"Okay, right," Aaron said as he gently pushed me away before raising his right arm, wrist upwards, towards his mouth. I pushed it away just as his fangs flashed under his soft, full lips.

"No!"

"What the... Bea, what are you doing?"

"If it's got to be done, he can have mine."

"What the hell, Bea! You can't do that. You know what will happen."

"I do. I know full well and you should be happy; at least we'll be together forever and I'll never lose my dad ever again. It's the only way I can do this; I need you to draw my blood."

"I can't, Bea. It can't be this way."

"Well, if you don't do it, I'll just cut myself – would you rather me do that?"

"No. No, don't you even….."

"If I cut myself, I won't be able to stop the blood. If you bite me, it can be controlled."

"I know that, Bea and that's not what bothers me, but," Aaron stammered, "you give your dad your blood and that's it, there really is no going back."

"I'm more than aware of that," I replied firmly, "and if saving him turns us both immortal then that's just the way it has to be. It's a win-win situation." I looked at Aaron lovingly and from the look on his face, he knew straight away what he had to do.

"I love you, Beatrice Harvey. Here's to immortality!"

Chapter 26

Aaron bit hard and deep and although I felt pain, it was good, very good. He kept his mouth on my wrist, stemming the flow of blood with his tongue. I looked down at my father, sincerely hoping he didn't wake up at the same moment I thrust my wrist to his dry, gaping mouth. He did though and I immediately placed my wrist over his open mouth, letting a few drops fall before going any further. His dehydrated tongue flicked and rolled, his eyelids twitched. I shoved my wrist down, covering his mouth entirely. He struggled a little but then fed like a hungry baby, holding my wrist tightly.

After a minute or so, I started to feel lightheaded and I looked at Aaron, silently hoping he would rip me away but he just shook his head at me.

"Not yet, angel; don't worry, I promise to stop him in time."

I nodded, feeling reassured but none the less drowsy. Then the pain hit; it was as if my father was drawing the blood straight from my heart. Spots flashed in front of my eyes and my body felt completely weightless. I was going to pass out, or at least, that's how I felt. Was I turning or did I actually have to die first?

"Okay, that's enough!" I heard Aaron shout. It sounded like I was under water and he was shouting the call from the shore, "That's enough, Mr Harvey, stop!"

That was the last thing I heard as a human.

Chapter 27

You hear so many near-death-experience stories on documentaries and such; some people have said that long passed members of their family met with them; others said they gravitated towards an intense white light. None of this was evident to me. Was I in limbo? Was this the world between worlds? Nothingness surrounded me; pure nothingness. That's the only way to explain where I was. I felt like a will-o'-the-wisp, flitting and floating around in a place I couldn't get out of.

All of a sudden, it felt like I was being smothered. I tried to scream but no sound came. I felt more pressure on my mouth and then a drop of liquid trickled past my lips and down my throat. It tasted so good. It refreshed me. Then a deluge of it gushed and I gulped greedily. What the hell was happening? How could I feel all of this if I was dead?

Soft, muted colours began to appear; it was like there was a pastel picture being created right in front of my eyes. Then I heard muffled yet rich noises; someone was talking. I wanted to talk but nothing was happening. The liquid stopped, the sound disappeared and once again, I was immersed in nothing.

"Bea, honey, come on – please! Please wake up. You have to come back. I need you."

My eyes flickered open and Aaron's face filled my vision. I opened my mouth to speak, actually no, to scream; I wanted to scream out how much I loved him but all that came out was a rough, ragged, rasping sound. Aaron threw his arms around me, gathering my body up into his embrace. I could feel him shaking; he was crying.

"Bea!" he shouted, "thank God. I thought I lost you."

Something weird was happening. Aaron always smelled amazing but this was different. Not only could I pick out his usual aftershave, shampoo and conditioner, I could smell his emotions. I could smell happiness and relief. I breathed it all in; I let it completely consume my senses as I closed eyes. After a moment, my voice made its debut.

"Aaron," I croaked.

"Hey, shush – its okay."

"Aaron, what happened?"

"It's all okay, honey. Don't worry."

Strangely, I didn't feel worried at all; far from it. I did, however, want to know what the hell I had just gone through.

"I'm okay," I said, starting to sound more like my usual self, "I promise. I'm fine."

Aaron gently pushed me out of the hug and looked me up and down. He stroked my face tenderly as tears streamed from his eyes. He exhaled loudly and it was easy to hear the tremble in his voice.

"You sure?" he asked. I nodded.

"Did I die?"

"We all do," he answered.

"No shit, Sherlock…."

"And she's back in the room," he interrupted. I smiled at him.

"Look, just tell me what happened okay?" I asked.

My father was coming to, fidgeting and moaning on the bed he was dying on not so long ago. Aaron followed my gaze and looked over at him.

"Let's keep our voices down a bit eh?" he asked quietly, "he's not quite compos mentis just yet if you catch my drift. Let's not scare him with the gory details the moment he wakes up." I nodded again.

"Well, go on then," I whispered urgently.

"Your dad, to put it simply, drained you dry," Aaron said, "He took you too far."

"Too far as in…"

"As in you wouldn't have come back of your own accord," Aaron continued, "I'm really sorry, Bea. What little blood I gave you the last time was just enough to bring you back but clearly it was not enough to protect you this time."

"So, what you're saying is," I said sharply, already guessing what his response would be.

"You were dead for too long, honey. I didn't want to give you my blood again but I had to. I so wanted you to come back on your own." Aaron said, dropping his head as he choked back tears.

"Hey," I said, squeezing him tightly, allowing my face to sink into his mop of hair, "I wanted this. I knew I would turn once Dad fed from me. The fact that you turned me means so much more than just coming back on my my own."

"I just did what I thought was best, that's all I could do," he said, not even trying to hold back his emerging sobs.

"Of course you did and honestly, Aaron, this is for the best." I hoped my assurance was enough to drown out his guilt.

"You drank a lot," he said as he raised his head to look at me.

"I did?" I asked, worriedly, "Are you okay then? Have I done any damage?"

"I'm afraid there's no getting rid of me, Bea," he answered, smiling sweetly at me.

"See, we're all cool then?"

"I guess so."

It was abundantly clear that Aaron was not okay but his guilt was purely self-imposed. He did what was absolutely necessary. The alternative scenario was one I didn't even want to imagine.

We were engrossed in each other; lost in our own little world. There was nothing or no one else that mattered and for the second time, we forgot about my father until he shot up on the bed like a rake that had been stepped on. He took a sharp, deep breath. I got up quickly and ran to his side. Aaron followed instinctively.

Even though I just wanted to hold my father, tell him how much I loved him; tell him everything, Aaron was right. He needed to take a little time to come round. After a minute or so, my father was ready to speak.

"Beatrice," he forced out, "what happened? What's going on?"

It wasn't the best time to tell my father that he had, not too long ago, fed on the blood of his only daughter. Somehow, I didn't think he would appreciate it.

"Shush, Dad, just relax. Everything's fine."

Chapter 28

My father didn't speak; he just stared into space while I explained what had happened. He shook his head in disbelief but he also knew that I was being totally serious.

"Why, Beatrice?"

"Why? Because I love you, Dad."

"I love you too, my darling but you should have let me go. It was my time."

"No! No it wasn't. I need you, Dad."

"Beatrice, I love you more than anything in the world but this is not right and do you know what upsets me even more?" he said and I knew exactly what he would say next, "the fact that you did it. You turned me. You gave up your own mortality to save someone who really shouldn't be here. Do you think that makes me happy?"

I couldn't answer him because I guess it was pretty selfish of me, very selfish actually, but I turned my father for the right reasons, well at least that's what I believed.

"But, Dad...."

"Beatrice, I know why you felt you needed to *save* me but you really haven't, and you," he said, looking straight at Aaron, his face twisted with anger, "you should be disgusted with yourself. You should have talked her out of it. You should have stopped her."

"Dad, don't you dare…"

"Don't defend him, Beatrice. He had no right to turn you too!"

"So he was just supposed to let me die as well?"

"Well, no but if you hadn't made this ridiculous decision to bring me back, there would at least still be one of us alive; one of us still mortal."

"Mr. Harvey," Aaron jumped in, "I completely understand why you detest me right now but you know your daughter, we both do. We know how strong willed, determined and stubborn she is. You may not want to believe this but I did everything I could to discourage her. I ask you the same question you asked Bea; do you think this makes me happy?"

My father fell silent and I felt so sorry for him; it was all too much to take in.

"Okay, I suppose I can appreciate that, Aaron," he replied, "but you two will be together forever now. Who do I have to spend my eternity with?"

"You have me, Dad!" I answered.

"Yes, and that's just great, Beatrice, it is really, but I have no one to spend my days with. I haven't anyone to love, to lie with, laugh with, be with and it's not like I can go and find myself a woman now, is it? You and Aaron don't have that to worry about."

There really was no argument; he was right and I felt sick to my stomach because of it. I had seriously made a total mess of everything. What had I done? I started to cry. Aaron put his arm round my shoulders and kissed my head.

"Beatrice, listen to me now," my father said as soothingly as he could manage, "what's done is done. There is no backing out of this now."

I looked at my father and then back to Aaron who nodded in agreement with my father. After a moment of contemplative silence, my father started to retch and cough.

"Dad!" I shouted as I rushed over to him, "What's the matter? Are you okay?"

"You see," he said between moans of pain, "this is what you didn't factor in to all of this, Beatrice."

"What, Dad?"

"I'm hungry. I need blood. I have to feed. What am I going to do now? Actually, no, correction – what are you going to do about it?"

I looked to Aaron, following the direction of my father's gaze. Aaron was stoic and unperturbed.

"Mr. Harvey, please don't panic."

"Don't panic, Aaron," my father shouted back, "do you know what I want to do right now?"

"I'm more than aware of what you want to do, Sir." Aaron answered.

"Don't come the smart Alec with me, son. What I want to do, what I need to do is get out of here and feed and that means I have to end someone's life. That disgusts me. Does it disgust you?"

"Yes, it does," Aaron replied, "which is why we have

a supply of blood bags on the bus."

"And when those run out?"

"They won't. We have contacts in hospitals in pretty much every city of every country in the world. When you've been around as long as us, you get to know the right people. You will feel you *need* to feed from the source for quite a while but it does pass and then drinking blood from the bag will just become second nature."

"I sincerely hope you're correct, Aaron," my father said, shaking his head.

"Can I ask a question, Aaron?" I said quietly.

"Of course you can, honey."

"Why don't I feel hungry? Why don't I feel exactly the same as my dad?"

"Bea, you drank so much from me that it quelled your appetite. You should be fine for twenty four hours at the very least. You'll know when you need to feed, just like your dad. I'm afraid you haven't got out of that."

"Oh well, never mind," I said sarcastically.

"Anyway, Mr. Harvey," Aaron said, turning to my father, "we best get you back to the bus and get you sorted, okay?"

"I think that's the best idea you've probably ever had," he replied scathingly.

******

We helped my father pack all his belongings in total silence, knowing we would get snapped at if we spoke any more of the day's events. Aaron text Jim, explaining that we were ready to go, and within thirty minutes, he was knocking on the door. I opened it to see an out of breath, red faced Jim, staring back at me hopefully.

"Well, did everything go okay?" he asked.

"I suppose you could say that," I whispered, "if by *okay* you mean turning your own father and being turned in the process, then yes, everything is just peachy." The look of hope in Jim's eyes quickly turned to that of concerned pity.

"Oh, Bea," Jim whispered back, "I'm so sorry sweetheart."

"It's okay, Jim, really," I replied, "it's my dad we're more concerned about."

"He's hungry, right?"

"In one," I replied.

"Okay, chick, let's get this show on the road," Jim said as he looked past me to Aaron and my father who were standing at opposite ends of the bed, "Mr. Harvey, Aaron – I think it's time we all go."

Jim held the door open for the three of us and we filed out. All I could hope for was getting out of that place and on to the bus without my father wanting to sink his teeth into the first person he saw.

Chapter 29

We damn near raced to the taxi. Jim's face dropped as we noticed a Parking Attendant grilling the driver.

"Hey hey, what're you doing, man?" the taxi driver shouted, in almost perfect English albeit with a Danish twang, at the traffic warden who had just popped a ticket under the left windscreen wiper of the cab. "I only went over the road for five minutes. I needed to get some cigarettes."

Jim shook his head. It was contagious.

"This is a no park zone, Sir," the warden explained.

"I wasn't parked up," taxi-driver said, quieter this time, trying to reason with him.

"No, he wasn't," Jim added, "he was waiting for the four of us." Aaron and I nodded fervently, hoping to emphasise the point.

"Four?" the warden said, looking around, "Don't you mean three? Not that that should make any difference in the matter. Sir," he went back to taxi-driver, "this is a drop off and pick up point *only*. You cannot park, no matter what your story is."

As if a switch had been flicked on in our heads, Aaron, Jim and I turned to look behind us and at precisely the same time, realisation hit; my dad had gone.

"Oh my God," I shouted, pulling at my hair.

"Where the hell…."Aaron joined in.

"Oh man, this really isn't good," Jim added, stating the blatantly obvious.

"Oh, you think, Jim?" Aaron replied sarcastically.

"For God's sake you two, this is not helping at all," I shouted over them.

"She's right," Jim said, grabbing my hand tightly, "come on, let's get off."

"How, Jim?" I asked and in perfect timing, the warden piped up.

"Excuse me but I'm sorry, you cannot go anywhere until the driver has paid his fine. Once it's done, you're free to go."

We all looked at the taxi-driver who looked back at us in stunned silence.

"Well, are you going to pay it then, mate?" Jim said.

"I don't see why I should have to," he replied, "Where's the sign? Where is the sign to say I can't park here?"

"Sir, you are a resident of Denmark, are you not?" the warden asked.

"Yes, but….."

"Is this for real?" Aaron shouted, "Pay the bloody fine! We have an emergency here, mate. If we don't go and find our friend, the shit's going to hit the fan!"

"But I….." taxi-driver said, trailing off.

"Here," Jim shouted angrily as he delved into his trouser pocket in search of his wallet, "I'll pay the bloody fine; how much?"

"Sir, it really isn't your business to pay the debt owed by the driver," the warden explained.

"I know that, mate, but he's dragging his arse and we

don't have time for his shit. Now, how much is it please?"

"Five hundred and ten kroner, Sir," the warden answered, "you will be compensated for this. Now if I can just take your details….."

"There you go, mate," Jim said as he slammed the money into the top pocket of the warden's high visibility shirt, "Take it. Like I say, we don't have time for this. We're going."

The look on the warden's face was a picture; if the situation wasn't so serious, I would have fell to the ground laughing.

"We'll be in touch with you, Sir," the warden said to the driver, "you will have to pay double, plus interest, so we can compensate the gentleman that paid *your* fine for you."

The driver said nothing; just nodded. He got in to the driver's seat and we all piled into the back. None of us spoke. It seemed clear that if Jim did, he would have unleashed hell on him. We were all in silent agreement that we just needed to get the hell out of there and try to find my father.

"He can't have got that far, Bea," Aaron said, putting his hand on my shaking knee, "he's not long been turned so he'll be disorientated and confused."

"You know that, do you?" I said, knowing how desperate my father was to feed.

"We'll find him, guys," Jim said, trying his hardest, yet failing to sound positive.

"I bloody well hope so," I said, "let's pray we find him before he kills someone."

"I'm sure it won't come to that," Aaron said, looking as unconvinced as I did.

Looking away from him and out the window, I hoped beyond all hope that the first thing my eyes would see would be my father, standing on a street corner, looking bewildered. No such sight met me though and all I could feel was guilt; guilt and sadness. It was all my fault. I should have let him go. I knew, in my heart of hearts that my father would never have allowed this - would never have let me entertain the idea. I struggled to hold back the tears that were threatening to cascade from my tired, sore eyes and just as I thought all hope was lost...

"There he is!" Aaron shouted, almost deafening me in the process.

"Stop!" Jim shouted at the driver who slammed on the brakes, throwing the three of us forward. I turned my head and looked in the direction of Aaron's outstretched arm and pointed finger.

Sure enough, there was my father across the street. He was sitting outside a comic book shop; knees drawn up into his chest with his arms wrapped around them. His head was between his knees.

Aaron hit a button and his window slid down automatically.

"Mr. Harvey!" he bellowed out into the street. My dad did nothing in response, "Mr. Harvey, it's me, Aaron. Beatrice is here too."

He definitely heard Aaron this time. The relief I felt was immense; my immortal heart felt like it would explode from my chest in pure elation. The feeling quickly dispersed though when I saw the dried, encrusted blood around my father's grinning mouth.

Chapter 30

Aaron flung his door open, holding me back with his free hand, obviously wanting to stop me from fleeing from the car to get to my father.

"Aaron, he's my dad!" I spat angrily.

"Just stay where you are," he said firmly, "believe it or not, you'll thank me for it."

He ran across the wide road, dodging cars and cyclists swiftly and easily. Watching him manoeuvre so fluidly made me hope I would inherit his gracefulness and speed. I lost him, just for a fraction of a second, as a lorry lumbered past and then he was standing in front of my father, trying to coax him into getting up.

After a small fracas, my father got up and allowed

Aaron to drape his arm over his shoulders, guiding him back to our taxi.

I could barely bring myself to look at my dad as he reached the car. He looked damaged and deranged. He wasn't the man I knew and loved but what the hell did I expect?

Aaron seemed to sense my repulsion, opened the front passenger side door to let Jim out and bundled my father into the seat before climbing back in next to me. As Jim sat down to my other side, he really didn't know where to look; his eyes flitting everywhere other than where my father was sitting.

"Right, we all ready then?" Jim asked, tapping the driver's shoulder, "Okay then, mate, off we go," he continued when he received no answer from our terrified escort.

"Jim, we need to cancel the gig tonight," Aaron stated firmly as he slumped on to the settee on the bus. We followed suit. I didn't put up an argument this time; he was right. He looked at me, expecting me to tell him off, "Bea, I don't care what you say this time, we cannot play; there's too much shit gone down today. We need to get this sorted." I nodded. He smiled sweetly. I couldn't say no to that face.

"And it's not just that, honey," he continued, "you'll definitely need to stay away from the crowds tonight.

Even though you've had your fill from me, once you see all those fans; hear their blood pumping in their veins, you won't be holding back, not this time round."

"He's right, Bea," Jim interrupted, "and we definitely can't leave your dad. He's got the taste for it now; blood from the source, not from those bags in the fridge. His urge will be even stronger now and he won't think twice about breaking through locks, doors and whatever else stands in his way."

The three of us looked at my father who was laughing insanely, sitting cross-legged on the floor with his back against the fridge. All I wanted to do was grab hold of him and shake him until he stopped.

Chapter 31

The management at Train was not at all happy with the last minute cancellation, and understandably so; notifying them with only a few hours to go was a big problem. I felt incredibly guilty but at the same time, I knew it was the right decision. I did not envy, not one little bit, the person who had the task of letting the fans know. Aaron had arranged a future date with the guy in charge who had made it perfectly clear that if Shout the Call cancelled a second time, they would never again cross over Train's threshold.

"So when's the new date then, mate?" Jim asked Aaron.

"Next Friday," Aaron answered, "it'll give us a whole week to get Bea and Mr. Harvey used to the stash in the fridge." He looked at me apologetically.

"That's not enough time, you know it isn't," Jim said, visibly concerned, "Look at how long it took you, mate!"

"Well, we're just going to have to work extra hard then, aren't we? I couldn't turn the date down; it's all that was offered."

"No, you couldn't," I shot in, "Jim, Aaron couldn't let Train down, you know he couldn't," I said, turning around to face him and looking deep into his eyes, "I promise I will do my very best to *not* rip someone's throat out." I was hoping the hint of humour in my tone would lift the atmosphere but only Jim saw the funny side. I looked over at my father, silently pleading with him to make a promise too. He was silent but for the menacing little giggle that made his shoulders tremble. It was clear he wasn't about to promise anything to anyone.

"Dad, this is really important. Promise me; promise all of us that you'll at least give this a shot. I know the last thing you would want to do is kill someone, again." My father laughed.

"Ordinarily, Bea, you'd be right, that would be the very last thing I would ever want to do but as I have already said, you took my choice away from me. You and that," he pointed at Aaron, "you made me this way. He made you this way. I bet we don't manage the week."

"So you're not even going to try?" I asked angrily.

"Did I say that?" he replied. I flung myself at him and hugged him tightly, "Beatrice, no matter what has happened to us, no matter what we are, you are my daughter and I love you more than you could ever imagine. I will try, for you, but don't ask me to make a promise like that because I can't guarantee I'll keep it. I fed and I thought it would repulse me. I thought I would be disgusted but I wasn't and I loved it. Maybe there's more hope for you. You've only had Aaron's blood and now you're back here, ready to drink from the bag. I sincerely hope you manage to sustain without having to do what I did."

"Me too, Dad."

Aaron handed a blood bag to me and one to my father. "You want glasses?" he asked.

"Why, will that make it taste even more amazing?" my father asked back sarcastically. Aaron shook his head. I held my bag up to my father's and we bumped them together as if they were, indeed, glasses of wine.

"Oh well, bottom's up," I said, trying to remain cheerful as I heard my stomach almost growl with hunger. I watched my father place the tube of his bag to his lips and I did the same. He closed his eyes and I did the same.

Blood flooded my mouth as I sucked and I gagged a

little as I tried to swallow the cold, slightly thick, iron tasting liquid. The first gulp didn't go down brilliantly but that soon changed. How could something so disgusting be so incredibly delicious? I drained my bag in no time, opening my eyes just as the last drop crossed my lips, so as I could see how my father was getting on. He wasn't getting on; not at all. He'd barely taken a thimbleful.

I can't do it," he said, looking like he was close to vomiting.

"Yes, you can. You must, Dad." I said, willing him on as he put the tube to his mouth again, closing his eyes. He chugged down the blood.

"There, you see. You did it!" I said proudly, "Dad, are you okay?"

My father was a pallid grey in colour; he looked awful. Sweat beaded on his forehead and top lip.

"That's not going to stay down," Aaron whispered to me out the corner of his mouth.

"He'll be fine," I replied but seconds later, my father bent over double, clutching at his stomach and vomited a waterfall of blood.

Aaron looked at me, much as if to say, *I told you so*. I looked at him in an *I'm-seriously-not-in-the mood* way.

I grabbed a roll of kitchen paper, got down on my hands and knees and started cleaning the deluge of deep red that seemed to have covered the entire bus floor. It felt like I would be mopping up blood for all of eternity. Slowly but surely, I cleaned up every last drop and sat next to my father.

"I'm sorry, Dad," I said, rubbing his back, trying to comfort him but clearly not making a great job of it.

"I knew this would happen, Beatrice," my father said apologetically, "How are you?"

"I'm fine, Dad. Well, I haven't bought anything back up anyway."

"That's great, sweetheart. I really think you'll do this."

He looked so sad. Even though my father knew drinking from the bag wouldn't help, I think, deep down, he wanted it to work more than anything. He got up from the settee and pulled his jacket from the coat hook on the inside of the bus door.

"Where are you going, Dad?"

"What I should have done in the beginning, Beatrice. I'm going home."

"What? No, Dad; you can't."

"I can and I must and I need to do it straight away. The sooner I'm gone, the better."

"No, you're wrong. We need to stick together. You know what you're capable of now and we need to make sure it doesn't happen again."

"That's why I'm going, sweetheart. I don't want you to see me feeding."

"You won't, Dad; you won't need to."

"Beatrice, I will. I'm too strong for you to stop me. I will do anything to get away from you and get to someone that will give me what I need."

"He's right, Bea," Aaron joined in, receiving a nod of agreement from Jim.

"But, Dad, please."

My father shook his head sadly and put on his jacket, smoothing it down with his hands.

"Beatrice, if I'm going to kill anyone, it most certainly will not be in front of my daughter. I know you mean well and I can see how much this is upsetting you but it really is the only way. Let me go. You'll never have to know anything then."

I started to cry. My father walked over to me and took me in his arms.

"I'm only ever a call away, sweetheart," my father went on, "we will always be family and you will always be my daughter. We'll still see each other, just not as often as we do now. Now," he said, pushing me away gently, brushing my tears away with his thumbs, "come on, everything will be okay."

He kissed my head, turned around and headed straight for the door. I felt Aaron at my side in a millisecond. He wrapped his arms around me and placed a kiss on my forehead just as the door closed behind my father.

Chapter 32

I cried for hours; until there were no more tears to cry. I felt physically and mentally drained. I couldn't have been any more grateful to Aaron for calling off the gig. I lay on his bunk whilst he talked to the rest of the band, informing them of the cancellation. From what I could hear, they all seemed pretty cool about it. I guess it was another night where they could go and paint the town red, unfortunately quite literally.

"Here you go, honey, get that down you," Aaron said comfortingly as he handed me a tumbler of whiskey.

"Thanks but no thanks," I replied indifferently, "alcohol is the last thing on my mind at the moment." He shrugged and placed the glass on the shelf by his window.

"I'll just leave it here in case you want it later. Do you want me to leave you on your own for a bit?"

No, I wanted to scream, *no I don't!* What I wanted, damn it, what I needed, was Aaron, preferably with his shirt off and kissing me all over. I didn't want him to leave me in any way whatsoever.

"No, please – stay with me," I answered desperately, "can we get out of here? Go for a walk or something?"

"Sure," he replied, "but we ain't going anywhere until you've knocked that whiskey back."

I sighed and rolled my eyes then did as I was told, throwing the whiskey back in one gulp. I winced as the fire burnt into my chest.

Aaron smiled at me and pulled me up from the bunk.

******

"So, apart from everything that's happened so far, how's Denmark treating you?" Aaron asked, trying to lighten the mood. It didn't and he was more than aware of the awkward, intense silence that followed.

"I'm sorry, Bea," Aaron sighed, looking glum, "I'm

sorry for trying to cheer you up. I'm sorry I had to turn you. I'm sorry you got this job. I'm sorry for everything!"

I stopped dead in my tracks, mentally and physically, and pulled Aaron backwards as he went to walk on ahead of me. We stood, facing each other, in silence. I wasn't sure if Aaron could feel the pent up sense of urgency between us but I could and it was electrifying. I pulled him closer still, grabbing at and holding on to the flimsy, soft material of his shirt. We kissed. It felt like our lives, albeit immortal, depended on it. The feeling enveloped me; my every sense screamed with need.

"I'm not," I said breathlessly as I briefly pulled out of the kiss, "I'm not sorry at all." I dived back in to carry on where we left off but Aaron pushed me away before it got too deep.

"That's good, Bea because it's me that has done this to you and I wish things were back to normal."

"What's *normal* anyway?" I asked, "I don't wish for anything other than what we have, Aaron - this is it now. I've only ever dreamt of being with you and now that dream has come true. What's even more amazing is the fact that now I know we'll never be apart; we'll never be alone. We will never be old. We'll stay this gorgeous for eternity." I laughed, hoping to inject a little positivity into the situation.

Aaron smiled sweetly.

"You say that now, but….."

"Stop! Not one *but* or *what-if* shall be uttered from now on," I shot in before he could finish, "I knew the consequences of saving my dad, which in hindsight, I really wish I could have just let him go, but….."

"You said no *but*'s," he said as pulled me to his chest and held me there tightly and I melted into his arms.

******

We walked back, hand in hand, lost in our own little world, all the way back to the bus.

The tour was headed to Germany next and we would be boarding the ferry at *Rodby Faerge* the next morning, and travelling a short forty five minutes to *Puttgarden*.

After all the excitement of the last twenty four hours or so, I just wanted an early night and even though Aaron hadn't said as much, I had a feeling he felt the same.

"What do I tell Hanley?" I asked Aaron as we slumped down on to his bed.

"About?" he said, realising how silly that sounded, "what I mean is, why tell him anything?"

"I need to tell him that I'm not *human* anymore. Somehow, I don't think New Music; Non Stop will look too kindly about having a vampire on their payroll."

"Bea, I've said it before but if you can control your desire for blood and use the bags, which I know you will do, Hanley really doesn't need to know a thing."

"Do the guys know?"

"I haven't said anything to them but I think they've pretty much guessed," Aaron answered, "You know what they say; it takes one to know one." I nodded – I guess he had a point. I kissed him and climbed over him to get off his bunk. I needed some time to myself but Aaron was in no mood to allow me that time as he pulled me roughly down on top of him.

"Where do you think you're going?" he asked, confused.

"To bed; I just need a bit of space. I think I might have a read for a bit or something."

"You can *read-for-a-bit* in my bed, can't you?"

"Aaron, seriously; just let me get my head together. No offence."

"Offence totally taken, Beatrice," he said, trying to be firm but failing as he broke into giggles, "are you implying that I'm an insatiable sex fiend?"

"Something like that," I answered, laughing along with him.

"What about if I promise to keep my hands and the rest of my body, to myself?" he said, clasping his hands over his lap, "Well, I'll have a go, anyway."

"I don't mind a cuddle and maybe a little kiss but then it's chill time, okay?" I broke into a smile.

"Yes, Miss!" Aaron said, cracking out that all too familiar smirk.

******

We arrived in Germany at twelve fifteen, and even though sleep felt like a best friend I would probably never see again, I raised my head from Aaron's pillow. As I gathered my senses, he plopped himself down beside me.

"Hello, sexy," he said, leaning forward, kissing me.

"Hey."

"So, have you missed sleep?"

"I'm not really sure," I answered, "I mean I've done

all nighters, hell, I've even done weekenders. I've gone without sleep on more occasions than I can remember so I can't say if it's much different to those times yet. If I don't hit the wall in a day or so, I'll know I've not missed it."

"Well, you'll find you grab sleep when you can, but like you've already seen, we go pretty much right through and sleep from about five am onwards. You'll find your time and you'll get use to it, honey, I know you will. You have to."

I pulled Aaron into a hug. He has this knack of saying exactly the right thing at exactly the right time.

"Look, it's a new day and a new place," he continued, "and a brand new life; not just for you, for the both of us. Now, I know you're still upset about your dad...."

"Well, I am but I'm not," I interrupted him, "I know he will kill, Aaron; it's in his blood now but at least, just like he said, I won't be around to see that shit. I think I'm actually feeling pretty optimistic."

"And that's a good thing," Aaron shot back in, "but you do know that if all gets a bit too much, if you need to talk about it, you just come straight out with it. You know I'll always be here."

I leant right up to kiss him.

"Wow," he said, taken aback, "what was that for?"

"Thank you. Just thank you."

"It's my pleasure, honey. Now, we've got five hours to fill," he said, peppering kisses down my neck, "is there anything in particular you fancy doing?"

"Oh, I could think of more than a few things," I answered suggestively, "but shall we start by trying to find a coffee shop? I could kill for a cup."

"And then?" he asked again.

"Well, let's just see what happens, shall we?"

"Sounds perfect."

******

Even though it hadn't been that long a break and it was only one gig that had to be cancelled, seeing and hearing Shout the Call play live again was exactly what I needed. The guys nailed it, as per usual. I checked through my photos, deleting the shoddy ones which thankfully weren't many, and found I had twenty minutes to kill before they all joined me backstage.

Aaron had already made sure there were enough blood bags to go around if we needed them; something I had never noticed before. I'd never even realised that the bags were always hidden behind all the beer, in all the fridges, in all the backstage rooms we had frequented so far. I already had an idea of how my interview with the band would pan out. I already knew I would concentrate a little more on the other guys, seeing as it only ever seemed to be Aaron that got interviewed. I pulled the fridge door open, grabbed a beer and cracked it open. I guzzled it down, enjoying the sensation as it flooded my mouth, savouring the lightly fizzy, hoppy liquid. My pleasure was quickly disturbed by the buzzing of my phone in my camera bag. I pulled it out and looked at the screen.

Bea, give me a call will you please Hun, ASAP? Cheers. H xxxx

Strange, I thought to myself. I hadn't heard one iota from Hanley for over a week. I wondered if the timing of his text was purely coincidental or whether, in some weird and almost inconceivable way, he had found out what happened. I mean, he'd already had dealings with my father; it was Hanley who had booked his accommodation and flights. My mind raced with question upon question, totally unrelated to the interview I was about to carry out and the only way to get answers was to make the call. Hanley picked up after the third ring.

"Bea. Thank God. Are you okay?"

"Um, yes, I'm fine?" I answered, wondering if he

believed the lie, "are you? You sound like you're freaking out."

"Oh yes, I'm good. So, you arrived safe in Germany then?"

"Yes," I answered, feeling an impending sense of panic wash over me, "why?"

"I need you to come back for a day or so, maybe a little longer."

"You know I can't do that, Hanley! I'm here for the whole tour, as you arranged. Jim will be furious if I leave now."

"No, Bea, he won't," he shouted, "He hasn't got a choice in the matter. He owes me so I'm sure he wouldn't mind letting you go for a while."

I could hear my blood pumping faster and faster as I seethed with anger; I could have cried with it.

"No, Hanley, I won't! I am here for the duration and I will not break a promise or a contract. If that's not good enough for you, I quit!"

"Beatrice Harvey," he said, sounding too much like my father, "Don't be so ridiculous. There's absolutely no need to be like this. In fact, I do believe you'll thank me when you get back."

"Thank you?" I said angrily, "You think I would thank you for tearing me away from this? No chance, Hanley; it's not going to happen!"

"Actually, Bea, it will. I've come in to some information about Shout the Call and they are seriously not what you think they are. They are far from the band you idolise."

"What do you mean, Hanley?" I said, throwing the red herring, "Because I tell you this, I'm doing nothing whatsoever until you tell me what the hell is going on. That's the deal; you tell and maybe I'll think about coming home."

"And that's the exact reason why I've booked a flight. I'm coming to get you, hon - you have no choice in the matter. I'm doing this for you Bea; I'm doing this because I care. You'll realise that when you're home."

Hanley hung up before I even had chance to offer up my last word. I threw my phone back into my open camera bag, jumped up from my seat and headed for the door. I had to get to the guys; I needed to be with Aaron.

Chapter 33

"Hey, calm down," Aaron said as I barrelled into him in the corridor, "what's the matter?"

"Hanley wants me off the tour, Aaron. I think he knows."

"What the…"

"I know. I mean, he didn't say it specifically," I went on, "but he knows. He said I would thank him for getting me out of here."

"Do you think your dad spoke to him?" Aaron asked, probably more than aware of the answer.

"He didn't say but that's what I think has happened and if that *is* what's happened, I will never speak to my dad again. I know he's not happy about any of this but he seemed okay in the end, didn't he?"

"Well, I thought so, yes."

"So, he's betrayed me then. Aaron, I can't believe it. Why couldn't he have just let me be?"

"I don't think he's done it out of malice, if he has done it at all," he said, "I mean, one of the other band members, and you know exactly who I'm talking about, may have got through to Hanley because he's jealous of a certain music photographer and reporter."

"Oh, man, I never thought of that," I said in dazed realization.

"It's a possibility, for sure," Aaron said, "I know Jack's putting on this front that he's okay with all of this, but you don't know him like I do. He can be a vindictive little shit and when he bears a grudge, he's like a dog with a bone."

"Okay," I said, trying to weigh all the factors up in my head, "but surely that means he would have had to implicate himself and the rest of the band? Surely he wouldn't have just betrayed you like that?"

"Well, I really hope it's not the case, just the same as I really hope your dad hasn't landed us in it," he said, "but the long and short of it is – someone has. To be honest, I don't care who did it. All I care about is getting you out of here and somewhere safe."

******

The motel was dark, dingy and seedy. It was just like one of those you see in the movies– a real cliché. The manager looked at us from behind his reception desk with suspicion. Bloody hell, did he know what we were too? After the briefest exchange, he handed us a room key and sneezed without covering his mouth. What a vile human being.

Aaron unlocked the door then lifted me up, cradling me in his arms.

"Have you told Jim what's going on?" I asked.

"I just told him we needed a bit of time alone together."

"And you told him where we would be?"

"Of course I did," he sighed, obviously irritated by my questioning. It looked like I'd managed to royally spoil the moment, "I called him before I ordered the taxi. Anyway, watch your head," he said as he carried me over the threshold.

The room was basic but it was clean. It had everything we needed; a double bed, bathroom and a large yet rather dated television. Aaron threw me on to the bed and immediately climbed on to me, straddling my hips.

"It's not a five star," he said as he kissed down my neck, "but it'll do."

I groaned with pleasure as his mouth found my shoulder, then my collar bone. I sat up, pushing him upright in the process, and took my top off. The look in his eyes screamed one thing and one thing only; he wanted me. I pulled his old, faded Iron Maiden t-shirt up over his head and threw it on the floor. His pecs flexed as my fingers ran over them.

I ran my hands upwards and let them get lost in his mass of unruly curls and then I pulled him in, kissing him deeply. With his mouth never straying from mine, he pushed me back down and trailed ever more kisses down my chest, stopping just at the waistband of my jeans.

We had been *together* like this before but now I was a vampire and Aaron was right when he said all my senses would be heightened.

******

"Aaron. Aaron, wake up," I said, glancing quickly at the bedside alarm clock – its illuminated, neon digits read out five forty five.

As far as sleeping goes, Aaron doesn't do much of it and as much as I hated waking him, there was no choice. Something or someone was outside our door.

"Please," I whispered, "please wake up."

"Wh-what?"

"There's someone outside," I said, holding the bed covers right up to my chin as if that in some way would save me if my life was put in danger. Aaron got out of bed. He was completely alert now. He stood at the door and put his ear to it, listening out.

"Who is it?" he asked, "Who's there?"

"Is that Aaron?" the voice asked. I knew who it belonged to immediately.

"Yes. What do you want?"

"It's Bea's boss, Hanley. Can you let me in please?"

Chapter 34

"Tell me what you want and I might think about letting you in," Aaron shouted through the door. It burst open and Hanley charged through before falling in a heap on the floor. He got up quickly and brushed himself down. If the situation wasn't so serious, I would have been howling with laughter.

"What the hell do you think you're doing?" I screamed at him, totally forgetting I was naked apart from a strategically positioned bed sheet.

"You're coming with me, Bea," Hanley replied, "but you knew that already."

"And I told you I wasn't," I said, grabbing my clothes from beside me on the floor and pulling them on under the sheets, "and that hasn't changed one bit since we spoke."

"You can put up as much as a fight as you want, sweetie," he answered nonchalantly, "but it won't stop me from taking you."

"She might not be able to stop you," Aaron shot in, "but I sure as hell will. Get out of here, Hanley before I do something I regret."

"Oh really, and what would that be then, lover boy?"

"Get out of here, Bea," Aaron said as he ran at him and tackled him back to the floor.

I didn't even attempt to slip my shoes on, I just did as he told me – I ran. As I got to the door, Hanley grabbed my right ankle and he pulled me to the ground.

My chin hit the floor with a crack. I felt it with the hand that wasn't trying to swat at Hanley – it didn't feel broken or too badly damaged. Maybe that was another benefit of being a vampire.

"Let her go, *now*," Aaron bellowed at Hanley. This only made Hanley more determined as he pulled me into his side.

"No, you let go," Hanley barked back.

Aaron tried throw a punch but wasn't in the position to put any weight behind it. Hanley was though, he caught

Aaron on the jaw, knocking him clean out. He pulled me sharply upwards and we stood there looking at my boyfriend lying broken and beaten, on the floor.

Chapter 35

We were questioned as Hanley man-handled me through check in and thereafter, on to the plane itself. He wasn't trying to beat me up or anything but I really wasn't making life easy for him. All I could think about was Aaron. We're immortal so I had no doubt whatsoever that he would eventually get up and wonder where the hell I'd got to. He would know, wouldn't he? He would know that Hanley had got his way and taken me.

After the flight and a long, mostly quiet car journey, we pulled up sharp outside the entrance to New Music; Non Stop. Hanley got out the car and made his way round to me. He opened my door. I looked straight at him but I couldn't speak. Don't get me wrong, I had words I could throw at him, *lots* of awful words but saying them would just make me even more angry; I had to try and keep my cool.

"Bea," Hanley said, "you won't believe me but I really have been so worried. Please, let's just get inside. We need to talk."

We got to my office. Why I actually have an office, I do not know. It's not like I used it all that often, most of my work's done on the hoof and then after hours at home. It felt alien to me - so far removed from my new life.

"Sit, Bea, please," Hanley said, gesturing to my rarely used chair. I didn't say anything, just sat down and watched him pull up a chair across from me. Rather than look him in the eyes, I stared into space, zoning out completely as he explained exactly what the members of Shout the Call were. It was all for my own good apparently; he would never forgive himself if he just went ahead and did nothing, not when he knew what they were.

"Hanley, just stop a second," I said, shaking my head as if doing that would shake all his words from it. He reminded me of one of those annoying little dogs with annoying little barks. Somehow, I needed to get past this irritation and break it to him that I was one of the *murdering-scumbag-bloodsuckers* he had just been speaking of.

"Sorry, Bea," he said, looking at me with such deep pity. I felt like slapping him round the face, "I know this must all be such an awful shock to you."

Nope, no shock at all, I thought to myself.

"Hanley, may I speak?" I asked, taking in a sharp, deep breath. *Here we go*, I thought. Hanley nodded so I continued, "I know you're only doing what you think is best for me, Hanley. I don't doubt that for a second but let me be clear about this; I know what the members of the band are."

His face turned pale. He looked like he had just seen a ghost.

"I know they are vampires," I went on, "I know Jim is too."

"Why the hell did you not come straight back?"

"I didn't want to."

"What the hell, Bea! You could have got yourself killed. What is wrong with you?"

"Hanley, the more you scream and shout at me, the less likely it is I'm going to talk. I'm a grown woman for Christ's sake; I make my own decisions."

"Well, it's lucky we got you back in time then. I'm sure it wouldn't have been long before one of them tried to feed off you."

"Ah," I sighed as I dropped my gaze to the floor, "well that's the thing you see, you didn't get me back in time."

Hanley looked like he was about to throw up all over his perfectly pressed designer suit. He laughed nervously.

"Don't wind me up, Bea; I am seriously not in the mood."

"I'm not winding you up, Hanley. It's the truth; I'm one of them."

He shot up out of his chair, knocking it over in the process, holding his head as if that would stop it from exploding.

"No, no, no!" he shouted, "I don't believe you. It can't be true; tell me it's not true!"

I nodded.

"The thing is, Hanley, even though I'm sure you've only done this to keep me safe, I really couldn't be in any more danger and as a result, I'm putting everyone here in danger too. You see, so far I've managed to fulfil my desire for blood by drinking from blood bags that the band always has on the bus. So far, I've not had to hurt, maim or kill...yet. It's not been long since I last fed so I'm sure you'll all be okay for a little while but, Hanley, I'm going to need blood sooner or later so unless you have a stash somewhere too, someone is, quite literally, going to get it in the neck."

"You, I..." Hanley stammered.

"There's something else."

"What? What are you going to enlighten me with now? Can you just shut up a minute? I can't take this all in."

"No, sorry; I can't. You need to know everything."

He covered his face with his hands.

"It's my dad," I continued on, regardless of what Hanley could or couldn't take.

"Oh God," Hanley said as he removed his hands, bringing them down onto my desk; it looked as if he was bracing himself against it, "Is he okay? I got him out to you as quick as I could."

"I know, Hanley and I cannot thank you enough. Actually though, I haven't seen him at all since I turned him."

His eyes grew wide like saucers and he laughed dramatically.

"Well this just all gets better and better!"

"I gave Dad my blood. He fed from me but he took far too much and that's where Aaron came in."

"The lead-fucking-singer? Bea, I know you have the world's biggest crush on him but.."

"Anyway," I stopped him, "Aaron bought me back."

"Oh, how very kind of him. What a gent."

"Hanley, I was dying and he did what he had to do."

"And I suppose you're going to tell me you're in love with him?"

I nodded firmly, sincerely.

"Oh, Bea," Hanley said, shaking his head in pity for me, again, "this isn't a movie; this is real life."

"I'm aware of that, Hanley," I replied, trying to keep my temper from boiling over.

"He doesn't love you , Bea. He obviously only wants you for one reason. He's led you right up the garden path, my dear, and I suppose you have eternity to realise that now, don't you?"

"You know absolutely nothing about him!" I barked at Hanley, shooting up from my chair in sheer anger, "and actually, right now you're just proving you know nothing about me too. I'm done talking." I turned my back to him and headed towards the office door.

"Where do you think you're going?" he asked, running up behind me.

"I'm getting out of here before I feel the urge to feed. I'm so, so angry with you right now, Hanley. I've never felt this angry with anyone. Hunger and anger do not mix so if you know what's good for you, you'll let me go before I murder *every single one* of you."

Hanley laughed.

"You, my dear, are going nowhere; nowhere at all."

He raised his arm high, fist closed. I shut my eyes tight, waiting for the blow.

Chapter 36

I woke on a cold, hard concrete floor and my head felt like it would split open with my next, rasping breath. The belief I had that vampires didn't feel pain, well, that was shattered again.

It took a second or so to come to and on regaining a little composure, I realised my hands were tied up behind me. I was in a basement; the only source of light coming from a ridiculously dim, dirty light bulb, hanging directly above me.

I could hear muffled voices and wondered whether they were real or if I was concussed. Maybe I was even going mad. I followed the direction of the sound and my eyes came upon a vent, just inches to my left, the cover of which was just about hanging on by one rusty screw.

I knew I couldn't do anything with my hands so braced myself against the pipe I had been shackled to, making sure I was steady. I kicked at the vent and it dropped to the floor, barely making a sound. The air that came out of it stank and was full of dust. I very nearly fell backwards as I recoiled at the stench, choking on the smell and the debris. The talking became a little clearer; was that my father I could hear? I closed my eyes, focusing in on the voices.

"You did the right thing, Mr Harvey," I heard Hanley say, "We need Beatrice here. Aaron and the band will come running and we will be waiting."

"You just wait a minute, Hanley," my father said, "I told you about Beatrice, about what had happened because I was worried about her. I *do not* want the band involved, especially Aaron. He had no choice but to do what he did even though I'm nowhere near happy about it. I may not particularly relish what we've become but it had to happen and as far as I'm aware, Aaron has done nothing but take great care of my daughter. I need you to tell me, Hanley; how long have you known?"

"What?" Hanley replied.

"That they were vampires? You hardly seemed surprised when I told you. I know you know. So, how long?"

"Long enough."

"Which is exactly how long?"

"Look, to cut a very long story short, I've known Aaron from the very beginning, one hundred and sixteen years ago."

"What? So you're a….." my father asked. I could hear the emerging realisation in his tone.

"In one. Yes Mr. Harvey, I'm a vampire. Come on, surely you must have guessed?"

Silence.

"Not just any old vamp though, no sir," Hanley went on, "I am the *Head Boy*. I was the one who turned Jim one hundred and seventy years ago. He was fifty four and working down the mines. Jim went on to turn Aaron, just as I asked but I needed a few more men so I left Aaron to find four other good-lookers to join our special little gang and there you have it – Shout the Call were made."

I practically choked, gagging on the iron-tasting bile that rushed into my mouth. I wanted to scream, to cry out but I held back. I had to listen on. My father cleared his throat.

"So, if you created all this," he said, "you must have known that Beatrice would also be turned, sooner or later and if that is the case, why have you bought her back?"

"Of course I did, you are exactly right," Hanley answered my father matter-of-factly, "I need girls; I need lots more girls."

"More girls?" my dad asked, "why more girls?"

"Come on, it doesn't take a rocket scientist now, does it Mr. Harvey. I want to create a new race of vampires and for that, I need girls."

I shook my head. Hanley wanted to build a new generation of vampires. Where would it end? Would he end up taking over the country, maybe even the world?

"But, if they're immortal, how can they create a new life?" my father asked.

"Look, I haven't got time to go in to all the details but they can. Female vampires are super susceptible when it comes to making babies and the gestation time for those babies is shorter than that of their human equivalents."

"Can you hear yourself? Just listen to what you're saying," my father said, "you cannot create a *new race* of pure vampires if they're all bloody babes in arms!"

"Ah, well now, because our babies are *born* as vampires, not made," Hanley went on, sounding sickeningly sure of himself, "they will grow and develop just like anyone else *but* once they get into their twenties, their development will slow down and eventually stop."

"Why that particular time?"

"Because, Mr. Harvey, I was created in my twenties. I created Shout the Call in and around their twenties *and* I make absolutely sure that if any of the boys need to feed, I ask them to steer clear of any girl under the age of eighteen so that if they do perchance think they're worthy of being turned, it keeps everything in the balance I strive for."

I slumped to the floor. *So when Aaron and I finally decide to actually do it, I'll get pregnant*? I thought to myself. We'd done pretty much everything but '*it*' so far and that's only because Aaron kept holding himself back. I mean, I know he held back at first because he feared he would turn me if he got too excited, but last night at the motel, it was the same. Maybe he was just so used to *not* going all the way? But, maybe he already knew about Hanley's horrid scheme? I hoped it wasn't the latter.

"The thing is though, Mr Harvey," Hanley carried on again, "Aaron's become far too attached to Beatrice, which means he'll never go out of his way to hunt other girls and that's the reason why I'm holding Bea. I'm sorry, Mr. Harvey but I'm afraid your daughter is now surplus to requirements. She needs to be taken out of the equation because as long as she's in Aaron's life, my little army will never grow. I thought that once he had had a taste of Bea's blood, he would never touch those stupid bloody blood bags again and go out and hunt, but it's actually made him determined to try and live his immortal life without the need to harm anyone else. That means he won't want to turn anyone and that is definitely not the way to build an army now, is it?"

"So, you're going to kill her?" my father shouted in angry disbelief, exactly mirroring what I was thinking.

"There you go, that wasn't so hard was it?" Hanley replied, sarcasm evident in his voice.

"Are you crazy?"

"Yes, very much so; great, isn't it?" Hanley answered, laughing.

"You will not kill my daughter; you'll have to get past me first."

"Oh, hang on a bit," Hanley continued, still chuckling, "you think it's me that's going to do it? Oh dear, how funny. No, no I'm not. That's really not my style anymore. Why have dogs and bark yourself? Nope, I won't be doing any of the dirty work. I have never ever killed a fellow vampire in all my years as one and that's not about to change. I won't be the one to kill my beautiful Bea."

I felt even sicker; as if I would vomit at any given second. A deep sense of dread washed over me. I knew exactly where their conversation was going.

"Who then?" my father asked, sounding as terrified as I felt.

"Don't you worry, Mr. Harvey – I'm not totally heartless," Hanley answered him, laughing even more. If I wasn't tied up in a basement, I would have happily ripped his throat out, "I can assure you it won't be you; certainly not. It will be Aaron that takes on the task. It will teach him a lesson; it will teach him I mean business."

Finally, I threw up, spilling out the blood tinged bile right on to the floor between my knees. My head span with visions of Aaron spiking me; ending me.

"Over my dead body!" my father shouted at Hanley.

"Easily arranged," Hanley shot back at him as I heard the crunch and squelch of bone and muscle and finally, my father's last, rattling breath.

Chapter 37

I couldn't see for tears. I couldn't comprehend that I had just heard my father being murdered. My heart felt like it was going to burst with sadness. I had done everything to keep him with me and now he was gone. I was incredibly angry and equally terrified. I needed to clear my head and focus but sobbing wasn't exactly going to help me fight for my life. I shuffled myself around taking in all of the room; I needed my wits about me. I spotted a work bench in the far corner and hanging heavily on the wall either side of it were stakes, a dozen at the very least.

On the work bench itself was a vice and clamped in it was a stake that had either recently been made or one that was still being worked on. Shit. There were enough stakes to finish me, the band and then some. A sudden bolt of realisation hit me; why wait? I could just imagine Aaron standing in front of me, crying; pleading with Hanley and it hurt, so much. I didn't want to see him that way. I would rather kill myself than have the man I love do it; I knew it would destroy him.

I somehow managed to wriggle my wrists free and the relief I felt was instantaneous. My hands felt as light as feathers. I made my way over to the work bench. As well as the numerous stakes on show, there was a file. I inched it, as quietly as possible, to the front of the bench. I laughed. A sense of achievement flowed through me; the only vampire to end my life would be me and I had taken the first step towards making that a reality.

******

"Well, well, well," Hanley said, laughing as he came down the stairs, "what do we have here?"

I shook my head in silence, amazed he had got down those stairs without me hearing a thing.

"What's the matter, Bea," he went on, "it's not like you to be lost for words."

He walked right up to me, his face barely an inch from mine. I dropped the file. What was the point in even trying now? I thought about Aaron as I stared past Hanley's evil, soulless face; at least I would get to see the man I love one last time before he rammed one of Hanley's stakes through my heart. Maybe Hanley was right; maybe it should only be Aaron.

"Come on, honey, what's on your mind?" Hanley asked again, irritated by my silence, "You can tell me; you can tell me anything. That's what I'm here for."

The thought of giving up had crossed my mind but at that point, rage filled my entire being. I had to fight. Maybe then he would kill me himself which again would totally put the kibosh on his perfectly laid plans. I dropped my head to my chest, taking a second to gather myself and work out what I was going to do. Hanley lifted my chin up with his fingers and leaned right in close. He was going to try and kiss me; I could feel it in my bones.

"I don't know why I ever let you out of my sight," Hanley said, breathing hard on my lips.

I continued to stare at the floor; I would wait for exactly the right moment.

"I should have kept you right here, with me," he continued breathlessly, "I've wanted you from the start Bea. There is no one quite like you; you are very special to me."

I nodded in silent, faux agreement, looking straight in his eyes. I was ready to go in for the kill with so much more than a kiss.

Our lips touched and in that instant, I would have happily welcomed death, again.

"Oh dear me, Bea," he said, tutting and shaking his head, "not good, this is not good at all. When will you ever learn, huh?" he said as he turned and picked up the frayed rope from the floor. He span back round and I winced as he back handed me across the face.

******

You know in the cartoons when a character sees stars after being slugged in the face? Well, there's nothing fake about it. It's real; it's just no one else can see them.

"What did you go and do that for? Look what you made me do" Hanley said, rubbing his knuckles for effect.

I spat blood at him.

"Get up!" he ordered.

I wasn't about to move a muscle, partly due to stubbornness and partly due to pain.

"Get the hell up, Bea!" he shouted.

I complied.

"Finally," he continued, "look, what I actually came down here for in the first place is to let you know that Shout the Call are well and truly on their way back home and I know how much you must be missing your boyfriend."

I remained silent. The less I said, the less I would give away and the more it would irritate him, which could be both a good and a bad thing.

"So I'll be back down here as soon as they arrive," he continued, looping new rope around my wrists, knotting it and pulling it tight, "let's try to *not* escape again, huh?"

Chapter 38

What little sleep I managed to get was fitful and uncomfortable. I woke to hear more voices from the floor above and I knew that one of those voices belonged to Aaron. I couldn't bring myself to go and listen through the vent; I was too scared of what I would hear. After a few minutes of worrying about what I would say to Aaron when I finally saw him; about how I would react, the door to the cellar creaked open and Hanley practically skipped down the steps.

"Did you sleep well, dear?" he said, "I came down to check on you a couple of hours after our little chat and you were out for the count. Trying to escape is tiring business huh?"

I just stared at him. That was all I could manage and

actually, I didn't want to waste my breath on a response.

"So, you know why I'm here, don't you?"

I nodded my head.

"Well, are you going to come upstairs with me? Your boyfriend is eager to see you."

I nodded again.

"Can you give me a hand please, Hanley?" I asked.

"What, you're not free yet?"

"Not for the want of trying," I answered quietly.

"Aw, come on then," he said as he untied the rope, "poor Beatrice."

He gestured for me to lead the way up the steps, which I did. I put my hand on the globed door knob and took a long, hard, deep breath.

"Come on, Beatrice, we don't have all day."

I turned the knob and sheepishly cracked the door open. Aaron stood there, right in front of me. His face lit up with the biggest, most beautiful smile I had ever seen. For a moment, I forgot that I was waiting to be killed but then Hanley pushed me sharply forward, ruining my daydream.

"Hey!" Aaron shouted at Hanley, "don't you dare fucking touch her."

"Whatever," Hanley answered, rolling his eyes.

"Come here, you," Aaron said as he averted his attentions from Hanley, straight to me.

I practically flew into his open arms. I buried my head into his chest and wrapped my arms tightly around his waist. I wanted his body to swallow me up whole.

He lifted my chin and I looked deep into his eyes.

I let my hands run their way up his chest and onto his neck, then up into his hair. I filled my fists with it. He leaned down. His face was millimetres away from mine. He kissed me; softly at first, then fervently. Again, I totally forgot Hanley, and the rest of the band for that matter. It didn't matter to me at all. The only thing that mattered was Aaron. I pulled away from the kiss, choking up with tears. Was he even aware of Hanley's plan? It certainly didn't seem like it; maybe that was for the best.

"I love you so much," I told him, holding his face in my hands.

"Oh, Bea," he said back, "I love you too. You're okay, right?"

"I am now," I answered sincerely. Of course, I was so

happy to see him but I knew the real reason behind all of this.

"Gosh, just listen to the two of you," Hanley interrupted, "I don't think I've ever witnessed love like it; tragic really."

"Tragic? There's nothing tragic about this," Aaron barked at him defensively.

"No, no; of course - you're right," Hanley said, "Bea, would you like to tell him or should I?"

Aaron looked at me, confused.

"What's going on, Bea?" he asked. I swallowed hard and felt sweat prickle my skin.

"Oh, for crying out loud," Hanley shot in again, irritated by my delay, "look, Aaron, you and Beatrice here have become far too close; you're too *into each other*. I sent her out to you, as you so eagerly asked because I knew you *wanted* her and I hoped she'd get you back into drinking again - back into doing what you were made for. I'd like to award you full marks for inducting her into our ranks but I can't! I'd like to say I'm happy that you've fallen head over heels for her, but I can't do that either. Your love for her does not help me, Aaron. How does your self-imposed blood celibacy, all in the aid of love, help to get us more girls?"

Aaron's face had turned from angry to guilty in a matter of seconds.

"Bea, I'm so sorry," he said, ignoring Hanley's questioning, "I know you must be feeling used and afraid. What Hanley says is true; you were sent to me with a condition."

"I know, it's okay," I reassured him, "I know what his plan is. I know why you had to send for me."

"No, Bea, just hear me out, please," he went on, taking a deep breath and pointing at Hanley, "regardless of whatever he tells you, the main reason I wanted you out on tour, well, I've already told you that and that is the truth. That's all that matters to me; you're all that matters to me."

I put my nose to his, biting his bottom lip and pulling it into my mouth; if only I could show him just how much I needed him; how much I loved him.

"Jeeeez, Louise," Hanley said, pretending to gag, "you two are sickening. Back to me now, okay?"

"Fuck you," Aaron spat at him. Hanley shook his head.

"So, as I was saying; you fell in love, scuppering any chances of you recruiting me a female-vamp-gang."

"Right, yeah; and none of the others can do that right?" Aaron asked sarcastically.

"Oh, sure they can do it, Aaron," Hanley answered, "but it's not them the ladies want, not really. It's all about you, kid; you do things to them before you actually do things to them if you catch my drift. They're like putty in your hands."

Aaron stared at him in stunned silence.

"Christ almighty, Aaron, do I have to spell it out to you?" Hanley asked, exasperated.

"I, I just…." Aaron stammered.

"Beatrice here needs to be disposed of. She's dead wood, so to speak and that is why I got you back."

The proverbial penny dropped in Aaron's head, the look on his face was enough to tell me that. His eyes began to fill with tears. He shook his head.

"You brought her back so you could stake her?" he said, his words seemingly surprising him.

"Correction," Hanley answered, directing a knowing smile straight at me, "so *you* can stake her. I knew you would come running as soon as you found out I'd taken her and you know that I would never have dragged you away from a tour for no reason."

I looked up in to Aaron's eyes and far from seeing more tears, I saw anger; they were wide and his jaw was clenched.

"You want *me* to kill my girlfriend?"

"Hallelujah!" Hanley laughed.

"Well, you're obviously more stupid than you look," Aaron spat, "because you know there's absolutely no chance in hell that's going to happen!"

"Oh really, we'll just see about that," Hanley said, starting to sound as angry as Aaron.

"No, we won't. Get this through your thick skull; no way! There is no way I'm doing it."

"You will, Aaron. You will because I'm the boss. If you defy me, I will have you destroyed in front of her. I will make her watch; I will make her see how a vampire dies. Don't make that the last thing she ever sees before I do the same to her; it's too cruel."

I was following this tit-for-tat between the two of them like a tennis match; a rally of words and threats that I was just about sick and fed up of.

It was like I wasn't even in the room; I felt like a piece of meat. And then I had a Eureka moment. There, on a table, right behind Aaron, sat a knife block. What it was doing there, I do not know but it was there and it was perfect. I lunged for it before either he or Hanley had the chance to stop me, I pulled out the largest knife and span around to see their shocked, ashen faces.

"Forget it – I'll do this myself!"

******

In lightning speed, Aaron knocked the knife out of my hand, catching it before it hit the ground. With his back towards me, he stood between Hanley and me, forming a physical barrier. He wielded the knife out in front of him, right at Hanley.

"If you want her killed, I ain't going to be the one to do it," Aaron shouted, "so come on you bastard, do your worst!"

As if on cue, the band surrounded me and it didn't take a genius to figure out why.

"Please tell me you're kidding?" Aaron asked, figuring it out too.

"Nope, certainly not," Hanley answered, "You see, they haven't betrayed me. They don't fall in love with their victims. They're doing the job properly."

Tears welled up in my sore, tired eyes. It was all so awful. Aaron started to shake with anger. I put my arms around his waist; a small yet intense gesture to let him know I was with him, still.

"Guys, seriously?" he asked, directing the question to Tim, Alex, Liam and Jack. Not one of them answered; they just all shook their heads. I could smell their guilt a mile off and it disgusted me.

"It's kind of poetic justice that the vampires *you* made will be the ones to finish the both of you. Very fitting," Hanley said, "unless, of course, you do Bea and Shout the Call will be as one again."

Aaron stepped right back against me. With his left hand, he stroked the outside of my thigh then took my hand and as fast as he had knocked the knife out of it moments before, he yanked me away from the band and Hanley, practically dragging me up the stairs leading to the first floor.

Even though Aaron knew how strong Hanley would be and how he could probably get through anything, he forced the ornate, mahogany dresser up against the door of the bedroom we had just fled into.

"It won't do much, honey," he said, "but it might just give us a little time to figure out how the hell we're going to get out of here before we're hunted down and killed."

The sole window in the room was barred from the outside, making it seem that once Hanley had got someone in here, they weren't getting out. Aaron took off his top, revealing his toned torso. He wrapped the material around his hand and lower right arm, and using his elbow, he smashed out the window. It seemed a breeze for him. He turned round to face me, deadly serious.

"If we don't try, we'll never know," he said before turning back round to the window, grabbing the bars with his hands, "you're going to have to get behind me on this one, Bea, literally; hold on to me as I push."

I didn't mind that one bit. I flung my arms around his hips and held on tightly, whether that would be enough to anchor him, I wasn't sure.

He inhaled deeply and as he exhaled, he pushed against the bars; not a quick, forceful shove, more a controlled heave.

"Damn it," he shouted, "it's not going to go. I can't do it."

"You can," I assured him, kissing his back, "you're not one to give in easily; that I know for sure. Just try again, come on."

He braced himself again and repeated step one. With my arms still wrapped tightly around him, I could feel muscle and sinew tighten and contract, the sensation making me shudder with pleasure. Talk about making the best out of a bad situation!

On the fourth attempt, with a primal scream and all the strength he could muster, Aaron broke the bars free of their fixing. He caught them before they had chance to fall on to the patio area directly below us.

"There really is no use, you two," Hanley said, slamming against the door; in all the drama of trying to get out, we never heard him come up the stairs, "you can't escape me."

"We have to jump, Bea, right now!" Aaron ordered as Hanley carried on battering on the door. I nodded. He pulled me in to him and kissed my forehead. "Honey, I just need you to know something. No matter what happens, I love you so much. I have never loved anyone, ever. You complete me. I'm not a monster when I'm with you."

"Oh Aaron," I cried, "I...."

The door flew open; we dropped to the floor.

"Bloody hell, thank God you're okay," said Jim as he jumped over our pretty pathetic barrier. Light streamed in behind him and he looked every bit the movie hero as he stood over Hanley's body, sprawled out on the floor. He was out cold but definitely not dead. Jim pulled out two stakes from the belt around his waist.

"Hurry up then kids, we've got some vampires to kill!"

Chapter 39

On the landing, Jim pointed to another room, its door closed. Aaron nodded, grabbed my hand and led me over to a third door. Jim mouthed *one, two, three,* and on cue, the doors were flung open. The house was eerily silent, the only signs of activity coming from the three of us. Hanley would wake up sooner or later and the band had to be around somewhere. Like us, they had only one thing on their mind; murder. I turned around, certain I had heard something on the stairs but, on investigation, i found nothing. I squeezed Aaron's hand tightly and in response, he turned to face me.

"You okay, honey?" he whispered.

"Um, yes; I'm fine. Just my mind playing tricks on me."

"Are you scared?" he asked again.

"A bit," I whispered, "I didn't think my emotions would get the better of me. I thought vampires would be immune to fear."

"Nope, not at all," he said, "we still feel fear, we just channel it differently. It's a challenge to us and we act on it in whatever way we need to. You're still very new to this, Bea so don't worry about being scared. You'll learn how to control your fear soon enough."

"You're not scared though, are you? You don't seem that fazed by any of this."

"Bea, I've had plenty of practice; I've been around a while. If you weren't scared right now, I'd be worried."

"Thank you," I said, immediately feeling better; just a little less freaked out.

"What for?"

"For just being you and for being with me when it matters the most; I love you so much."

Aaron beamed, forgetting for a moment, just like I had, that we were both hunters *and* the hunted.

"I love you too, so much but you're talking like this is the end. It's not. Hanley's no different to any of us, even though he likes to think he is. So, let's try and find them before they find us and we'll settle this once and for all."

I nodded as Aaron stepped cautiously into the room and in the very same second, hands grabbed my ankles and pulled me swiftly down the stairs.

******

"Bea!" Aaron shouted as he fled down them to be greeted by the sight of Hanley and the band circling around me. I could just about see him through the gaps between their bodies.

"Did you really think Jim, you, or anyone else for that matter, could kill me, Aaron?" Hanley asked. Aaron didn't answer.

"I don't know how many times I need to tell you but I am your creator; I am the boss here, so you know...."

"Fuck you, Hanley!" Aaron roared.

"Ooh, getting a proper little temper on you there, mate. Now, to Beatrice and to the job in hand," Hanley said as the circle opened up. Aaron was in my full view now. Hanley went on, "I am giving you one last chance, Aaron, kill her; get rid. If you don't then one of your wonderful friends will." He pointed to Tim, Jack, Alex and Liam in turn.

"Well, they're going to have to then because I seriously would rather die than do it."

"Fine, decision made then," Hanley said, "as long as she's gone, I don't give a shit which one of you does it."

"Stop; stop now," I shouted, "Aaron, I know you don't want this; hell, it's not exactly ideal for me, but…"

"No. No way, Bea!"

"Just listen to me please," I said, pleading to him, "I want it to be you who kills me, not any one of those guys."

Aaron shook his head, rocking from one leg to another.

"Hanley, could you please let us have some time alone?" I asked.

"Do you honestly think I was born yesterday, Bea?"

"Please!"

"Look, it isn't going to happen, honey. He does it in front of me or one of the guys will do it."

"Okay, okay," I spat at Hanley before looking straight at Aaron.

"Aaron, just come here," I said quietly.

He walked over to me, wringing his hands; his head bowed. I stood up and out of the corner of my eye, I saw Jim at the top of the stairs.

I turned my head slightly to the left to get a better view of him as Hanley and the rest of the band huddled around each other, whispering. Jim shook his head and put his right index finger to his lips. In his left hand was a stake; I knew what he was going to do. I nodded once at him and turned back to Aaron. I looked hard into his eyes and cocked my head in Jim's direction. Aaron's gaze followed the direction; he saw Jim, looked back at me and nodded too. He understood completely.

"This will break my heart, Bea," he said.

"I know, honey," I replied, "and I know I'll never ever be able to fix it but I want the last face I see to be yours."

"I'll never stop loving you, ever."

"Me too."

Aaron was playing along well but I knew that every word coming from his mouth was sincere. I pulled him into my arms and as I rested my chin in the crook of his neck, I could see that Jim was poised and ready for action. Aaron gently pushed me away.

"Here you go, Aaron," Hanley said, coming up

behind him, passing him a stake, "you heard the lady; it's got to be you – how adorable."

Aaron took a deep breath, raised the stake and put its tip just over my heart; a heart that felt like it would beat itself right out of its cage. He gulped and drew his arm right back. Hanley was practically salivating at the sight before him.

In the time it took me to blink back the tears welling up in my eyes, Aaron pulled up short and span around in Hanley's direction. My eyes followed.

Hanley stood there like a statue. His eyes were wide and his mouth was open as if he were about to scream, and as if in a movie, he burst into flames before our eyes. His screams were unlike any sound I've ever heard; high pitched squeals that hurt my ears. Almost as quick as he had ignited, the fire ebbed away and he crumbled to dust. Jim was standing behind Hanley's smouldering ashes; the ashes of a man I had once admired. The stake in Jim's hand was bloodied. He looked crazy, scared and happy all at once. The rest of the band stood behind Jim, shaking their heads. I ran straight to him, side stepping the mound of powdered remains, and threw my arms around him.

"Oh my God, Jim, thank you. Thank you so much."

Jim squeezed me, a little too tightly. Aaron headed over, making a point of budging past his band mates, if you could call them *mates* any more.

"Jim; what Bea says – thank you, seriously," he said, shaking Jim's hand before hugging the pair of us.

Jim turned around to Jack, Liam, Tim and Alex.

"Are you guys okay?" he asked.

"What the hell?" Aaron butted in, "Jim, they were on the cards to kill Bea if I didn't do it; I don't think they deserve any of our sympathies!"

"Aaron, these guys are your friends," Jim said, "What did Hanley do, eh, fellas? Did he brainwash you or something?"

"Something like that," Alex answered, completely devoid of emotion.

"Don't make me laugh," Aaron shot in, "come on Jim, do you honestly buy that crap?"

"Aaron, you don't know how persuasive Hanley can be, I mean, could be," Jim answered.

"Being persuaded to do something is a hell of a lot different to being brainwashed, Jim."

Alex and the others stayed silent.

"I know that," Jim said, "but I honestly don't believe these guys would ever want to hurt you, not knowingly anyway. I can't believe it. I won't."

Aaron shook his head but didn't say another word. Maybe he was just tired of fighting. Maybe he actually *wanted* to believe Jim.

"Right," said Jim, "let's get cleaned up and get out of here."

Our trusty bus was waiting at the end of the gravel driveway and I didn't even try to stop the sigh of relief that escaped my mouth. Aaron squeezed my hand and smiled albeit awkwardly. He still wasn't convinced his friends were being completely honest but he trusted Jim's judgment.

"I don't think I've ever felt so glad to see that bloody thing," he said, mirroring exactly what I was thinking.

"Right, let's try and finish what we can of this tour eh?" Jim called.

Aaron and I headed to the door first but he stopped us in our tracks.

"Carry on, you two," Jim called, "looks like the rest of em are dragging their backsides as per."

We watched as Jim casually walked back to the rest of the band who hadn't moved an inch.

"Something's not right," Aaron said under his breath. We both turned round instinctively.

"Get on the bus and drive!" Jim screamed at us as we saw the stake burst through his chest.

Chapter 40

"Jim!" I screamed as we raced towards his fallen body, lying scorched on the floor.

"You bastards," Aaron shouted as he ran back towards the house, following Tim, Alex, Liam and Jack as they scurried back inside, "come out now; show yourselves."

The complete strangers that were once Aaron's best friends in the whole world filed out and then surrounded us; the smirks on each of their faces were evil.

"What have you done?" I asked, still in total disbelief.

"What was needed," Liam answered.

"What the hell is that supposed to mean?" Aaron asked, just about holding back tears. Tim spoke next.

"Let's just say that Shout the Call needs a new image," he said, "we need to mix things up a bit, you know, and like Hanley said, we need to get rid of the dead wood. Jim was too soft, just like you are. He was holding us back and so are you; you and this whiny little bitch. You're no fun anymore; being in *love* is messing with your mind. I mean, hand on heart, when was the last time you really enjoyed the kill?"

"I've never enjoyed it," Aaron answered, "you know that."

"Exactly," Jack piped in, "just because you've gone off the *real deal* doesn't mean we have to. You're ruining everything for the rest of us."

"What the hell do you think we have the bags for?" Aaron asked, his eyes wide with anger.

"Oh, come off it – you know it's not the same. For a kick off, it's bloody freezing," Jack answered.

"So, anyway, let's get back to the main point again, shall we? That's why we want you gone too, Aaron," Tim cut in, "and if killing the both of you is the only way to sort this mess out then so be it. It's nothing personal, you understand, right?"

He looked over to Alex and nodded. In a second, Tim was right behind me, holding my hands tightly. Aaron shot towards me instinctively but his effort to distract Tim and save me was thwarted as he was knocked across the floor.

"Bea, I think I speak for the whole band when I say how nice it's been to have you on tour with us," Tim said, looking to Jack and Liam who both nodded in agreement, "so this really is kind of hard for me. I'm afraid it's a necessary evil though. Thank you so much for the great photos and reviews but it's time to say goodbye now."

He raised his arm, stake in hand, to strike. I closed my eyes, resigning myself to the fact that it was the end of the road. I didn't want to go, especially not now. Aaron and I had done pretty much everything possible to stay together.

We may not have been *together* for a long while but we'd been through enough to last a lifetime already and I wanted to live one hundred more with him. I couldn't quit now. I couldn't just give up.

Tim let out a strained, gurgled scream. I opened my eyes to see Aaron, his back towards me, facing the space where Tim had just been. Just as with Hanley, all that was left of him was a pile of smouldering ashes.

"Who's next then?" Aaron shouted out to the others, reaching out his hand and grabbing mine, pulling me swiftly to his chest, "Come on, who wants it eh?"

Alex, Jack and Liam stood in front of us in shock. Seeing their friend crumble right in front of them had certainly had the desired effect.

"Where are you going?" Alex asked as Aaron pulled me back towards the bus.

"Anywhere away from you," Aaron said through tightly clenched jaws.

"What about us? What about the band?" Liam asked, looking confused.

"What band?" Aaron shouted, "the band died the moment you killed Jim and then tried to kill my girl, oh and let's not forget what happened to Bea's dad."

"We didn't do anything; we didn't kill anyone," Liam said, pleading with Aaron.

"I don't give a shit what you did or didn't do. The fact is, you did absolutely nothing to stop any of it. You just carried on being the pathetic sheep you all are. So, that's it for the band, okay? But, it's the start of a brand new chapter for me and Bea. Try and stop us and I will happily kill all three of you, do you understand?"

They all nodded in unison and this time, I didn't argue with Aaron – there could be no band any more. There could be no more Shout the Call.

"So, what do we do now?" I asked Aaron as he climbed into the driver's seat and I took my place on the passenger side. He shook his head.

"Honestly – I don't know; I just can't answer that right now."

"I know, I'm sorry." I said, understanding that we both needed some time to process what we'd been through.

"Don't be silly, Bea. Please don't apologise, for anything. I'm just a bit lost for words."

I climbed over and sat on his lap.

"Let's just drive," I whispered into his left ear, "anywhere."

"We can't drive forever, Bea."

"I know but just for now, let's just get away from here; away from everything. I don't care where we go, as long as we go there together."

I leaned down and kissed his neck, which instantly made him tense up. He let out a shaky sigh.

"Can't it wait, Bea?"

"Not for long," I answered breathlessly, "but I suppose, just for a little while, until we can find somewhere to park up. I mean, you realise it's only the second time we've had the bus to ourselves."

I immediately felt guilty; could I have been any less tactful? Yes, we had the bus to ourselves but the circumstances that led to this new found freedom were not at all happy ones. I looked at Aaron's hands resting on my thighs, blinking back tears.

"Hey," he said, lifting my chin up, "don't get upset. You know I want you, I *really* do and I was actually thinking the very same. It's just going to take some time to get my head back together, that's all."

******

We had been driving almost two hours when Aaron found a field, completely empty, other than a tethered up horse at the very end of it. He rubbed his eyes, exhausted.

"You okay if we settle here then, honey, just for tonight?" he asked.

"It's as good a place as any," I answered.

"Cool. Right, time for a drink huh? I think we both need one, don't you?"

"Too right," I answered enthusiastically.

"Wine? Beer? Something a little stronger?"

"Wine please," I answered, "red, if there's any left."

"Coming right up," he replied, pouring us a glass each before bringing it over to the settee. "Now, let's get comfortable."

I got up from the passenger seat and made my way over to him.

"Here," he said, "drink up."

Although I'm not one to 'neck' wine, I didn't argue with him. I took a large gulp of the liquid and melted as I swallowed it back. "Yummy," I said, letting out a sigh of relief and contentment.

"Yummy indeed," Aaron agreed, savouring his drink as much as I was.

Suddenly I felt nervous, as if I was meeting him for the very first time. I gulped and wondered if my face looked as red as it felt. It seemed he felt as awkward as I did as he glugged down the rest of his wine.

He ran his right hand up my thigh and then put his arm around my waist, pulling me almost on top of him. With his left hand, he turned my face around to his.

I took in the view in front of me; the mess of brown-blonde curls, those large, blue eyes, his chiselled jaw and those seriously kissable lips. I couldn't look away as I realised his face was getting closer. He kissed me softly then upped the pace. I mirrored his movement, getting completely lost in him.

"I love you, Bea. I love you so, so much," he said breathlessly in between kisses.

"I love you too," I replied just as breathlessly as he pulled me down on top of him.

******

"What the hell was that?" I asked, quickly breaking away from him, positive I'd heard something outside the bus.

"Nothing," he breathed into my ear, "it's nothing."

I pushed him off me. He sighed with disappointment.

"Shush, don't you hear that?" I asked again.

Aaron sat up; listening intently to what was now complete silence. Once again, my overactive imagination was getting the better of me.

"You're right, it's nothing," I finally agreed with him, pushing him back down but that was it; the moment was lost. *Way to go, Bea* I thought to myself, *talk about ruining a perfect evening*. Then I heard it again, whatever "it" was; a kind of scraping, scratching sound.

"Look, there it is again."

Aaron's face appeared concerned; he had heard it too this time around.

"I'm going to take a look outside," he said, getting up and smoothing down his jeans.

"No, Aaron, don't," I grabbed his arm and tried to pull him back down, "please, you don't know what's out there."

"Bea, I think I'm pretty capable of defending myself. Come on now, what's the worst than can happen - I get pecked at by a seagull? Come on, honey, I'm a big, scary vampire," he joked as he let his teeth come down for effect, "neither of us will settle until I check things out. Feel free to come with me if you're not too chicken."

"Right behind you," I gulped.

Something silently and swiftly yanked Aaron upwards.

"Get inside," he shouted from above me on the roof,

"Get inside and lock the door." He let out a moan of pain.

I shut the door, bolted it, then sat down on the settee, letting my tears flow freely, and as I was busy being a *victim*, all I could think of was that Aaron was up there, fighting for his life while I was being a total coward. Yes, he wanted me to stay safe but I would happily die if it meant saving him; rather that than live for eternity on my own. I got up, took a deep breath and unlocked the door.

There was a ladder running up the back end of the bus. I ran for it and the second I put my foot on the first rung, flashbacks of my father doing the same thing, climbing up the ladder on the back of our camper-van, flooded my head. We had some wonderful holidays in that thing; such happy times.

I shook my head. The time for memories and melancholy could wait. I needed to focus on the task at hand. I was struck by how quiet it was because when I was sitting inside, being pathetic, it sounded like Aaron was getting ten shades knocked out of him. I gingerly peeped over the top of the bus and almost fell straight back down the ladder at the sight before me.

Aaron stood there, covered in blood. It was everywhere; splattered all over his face, in his hair, on his clothes and his hands were saturated. My gaze then found its way to the three piles of ash pretty much right in front of me. It didn't take a rocket scientist to figure who each pile belonged to.

"It's them, right?" I asked quietly. Aaron nodded slowly, looking completely numb, "Oh my God, honey," I continued, launching myself at him and holding him tightly in my arms.

"What have I done?" he whispered, sniffling into my shoulder.

"What anyone would have done; they were trying to kill you and no doubt they would have killed me too if you hadn't finished them. You've saved both of us. You should in no way feel any guilt over this."

"I know Bea. I know you're exactly right, and I know I've questioned your sympathy for them but I've known them forever. They were my best friends…"

"I know they were and I do understand but best friends don't do what they did, Aaron and you were right when you said there was something *not* right in all of this," I reassured him. He pushed himself out of my arms.

"I know," he said, "but it still hurts."

"Of course it does, sweetie, but they got exactly what was coming to them."

He nodded and pulled me back in to him.

"I'm sorry I ever dragged you into all this shit, Bea; I

really am."

"You didn't. I came of my own free will, more than happily actually," I said, looking deep into his eyes, taking all his blood-stained beauty in. It dawned on me completely then, that this was the man that I would be spending eternity with and nothing in the world could have made me any happier.

Epilogue

To say it's been easy to get over what happened all those years ago would be the biggest lie ever told but we have and we're closer than ever. Trauma changes your life completely, in our case it's definitely been for the better. It has tied us. We are stronger, together, because of it.

We moved back into Jim's just over a month after that night on the bus; we thought a little holiday was in order before we settled down properly and not only do we call this place home now, it's also where we work.

Welcome to STC Recordings, one of the only places in London where bands can lodge whilst recording. The ground floor is a dedicated recording studio; we kept the kitchen/diner as it was, apart from a lick of paint. The three rooms on the first floor and two on the second are standalone living spaces and are pretty much always full.

Aaron and I live very happily in our favourite room of the house – the cellar. It seems even bigger now and every time I plonk myself on the settee, I think back to the very first time he brought me down here. It still feels as magical now as it did back then and I couldn't imagine living anywhere else.

We're still in cahoots with the local hospital and our bag supply rarely dwindles. No one knows we're vampires; seriously, no one who comes here has even the slightest clue.

I'm still shooting and reviewing gigs but for STC Recordings' sister company, STC Music Reviews. Actually, we're just about to head out so I'm afraid I'm going to have to love and leave you.

"Bea, you coming honey?"

See - told you so; got to go. See you.

End

Thanks to:

Simon: *my other half - I love you more than you'll ever know.*

Molly: *in the words of Stevie Wonder, "you are the sunshine of my life" – I am so proud to be your Mummy!*

Mom and Dad: *my hero's without a shadow of a doubt; I am proud to be your daughter.*

Ella: *my Sister and the best, most awesome friend in the universe.*

Paul: *my brother-in-law, good pal and fellow lead singer **and** our newest addition,*

Max: *the most gorgeous little boy in the world (thanks for making me an Auntie, Sis!).*

Nan and Grandad: *I wouldn't be the person I am today without you both. We miss you so much.*

Paul Mills; *even though you're no longer with us, I can't begin to tell you how much of an impact you've had on me.*

James Josiah: *for being such a fantastic friend and helping me get this book out. It's a pleasure to be your mate.*

Nick J. Townsend: *for your support, friendship and for Shout the Call's amazing front cover. It's awesome, just like you.*

Southcart Books (Scott & Amy): *thank you for investing your time in me and our other local authors. You have given us a platform to get our work out there. Southcart Books forever!*

Alison MacConnell: *for taking the time to sit down and proof read this.*

Thanks also to: *BB and Key, Claire, my Soul'd Out family, Dotty-Lotty, Sharon & Elton (Bridgtown Social Club), Holly, Jan, Leigh and Nick, Marl and Steve, Lucy and Chad, Lisa and Mick, Pat and Stu, Stu, Nicki and Elsie, Tony, Lynne, Abbi and Heidi, Brad, Brandon and Ben. Thank you to each and every person that bought my last book, Good for Nothing and thank you for continuing to support me. You'll really never know how much that means to me.*

So I say "thank you for the music" *and bands that got me through the writing of this book; My Chemical Romance, Taking Back Sunday, Pearl Jam, The Used, Nirvana, Soundgarden, The Wildhearts, The Beatles, Fleetwood Mac, Billy Idol, HAIM, Bruce Springsteen, Darlia, Yeah Yeah Yeahs, Lana Del Rey, Jack Savoretti………(there are loads more but I think I would have to add a whole extra chapter to the book just to fit them all in!)*

A note from the author:

Its Lucy here and I just want to say a huge thank you for buying this book and giving it a go. I write because I love to and if I make even a little amount of money from doing something I enjoy so much, then that's one hell of a bonus.

I live in Walsall, West Midlands and share my life with our beautiful daughter, Molly, my husband, Simon and our Staffordshire Bull Terrier, Pringle. My parents (Molly's grandparents) are two of the most wonderful, loving, encouraging and supportive people ever (as were my amazing grandparents who I miss incredibly) and I am incredibly proud and honoured to be their daughter. My Sister (aka "Best Friend"), her husband Paul and my lovely nephew Max mean so much to me too.

Apart from writing, I'm a photographer (**www.lucyonionsphotography.com**) and a lead singer (**www.souldoutuk.com**) which means I'm always stupidly busy but that's the way I rock 'n' roll folks.

I hope you've enjoyed reading the book as much as I loved writing it. If you would like to find out any more about my writing and what's coming up next, you can find me here: **http://lucyonions.wix.com/lucy-onions-author**

Printed in Great Britain
by Amazon